D0898324

SECRET SINS

C.D. Reiss

Secret Sins
by
CD Reiss

Copyright © 2016

ISBN: 978-1-68230-693-2

Cover Art designed by the author

*Thank you to Jean Siska for help
with legal traditions and terminology.*

Also by CD Reiss

CHAPTER 1.

1982

"How old are you anyway?"

The guy asking had long strawberry-red hair and wore only shorts and a single sock. He'd tattooed a treble clef on his Adam's apple that started a symphony of notes all over his chest and abs. His name was Strat, and whenever his shirtless torso showed up in *Rock Beat*, Lynn went crazy trying to play the song he'd had drawn on his body. It sounded like crap.

"Eighteen, asshole," I snarled, letting loose a yard-long cone of cigarette smoke. I stamped out what was left of my cigarette. "You going to call or what?"

He and Indy snickered. I saw them look at each other over their cards. They thought they had my bra off next. They were wrong. Only two hands beat a full house, and if one of them had a straight flush or four of a kind, I was tits to the rail.

"I'll raise you." Strat tossed a ten in the center of the table.

We'd been going for four hours already. Indy had met me on the beach and, after a short chat, invited me to play poker. Yoni and Lynn were already in the hotel room for the possibility of a threesome, which was how I'd ended up on the beach alone. But poker? I could do poker.

My friends hadn't lasted long. Yoni and Lynn had passed out when they ran out of cash. Keeping up with a couple of cash-rich rockers who didn't know what to do with their first chunk of advance money was hard.

Indy/Indiana McCaffrey played guitar for Bullets and Blood. I'd met him on the beach first. I'd stayed cool even though he was completely gorgeous and charming, but when Strat came into the hotel suite, I almost had a coronary. I was a huge fan. I'd played their debut album, *Kentucky Killer*, for two weeks straight until Dad took my cassette. Took the Walkman too. I bought another of each but hid them.

"Call," I said, tossing in my ten.

Indy threw down his cards. "Y'all are too rich for me."

Indy had sun-kissed brown hair and a ginger beard. He was down to his skivs and a bandana around his neck, toned and tan from head to toe. I'd taken all of his money, and Strat and I had been pretty equally matched. Now I was going to break him.

"Too rich and too young," Strat said, popping a peanut.

Lynn coughed on the couch. Stretched.

God, please don't let her puke.

"I told you. I'm eighteen."

I don't know if I mentioned this. I wasn't eighteen. I won't say if I was younger or older. You can go figure it out.

Strat laughed. "Flygirl…"

Flygirl was a pretty common way to address a girl in the eighties, crossing race and geography, but I still felt as if it made me attractive to him. Strat chewed his peanut as if it had the mass of a pack of gum, chin up, looking at me in my bra. I felt naked.

I *was* naked, but I hadn't felt like it until his eyes swung around the curves of my body. I wanted to tell him to go fuck himself, but he finished before I could get a mental jacket on.

"You got a mouth like an old lady," Strat said.

His stare froze me in place. The backs of my thighs got sticky on the pleather.

"Never heard a girl talk like you."

Green was the rarest eye color, and his looked like precious Chinese jade.

He was so hot.

A hot rock star.

I put my cards down, snapping each one in the fan as I laid them out. "Aces full of sevens. You got anything in your hand besides your dick?"

Indy whooped. "She's got you, Stratty-boy. The pot and... what do you have left? Pants and a sock, bro. Go for the sock."

Indy was an amateur. He was beautiful and brilliant, but he didn't act twenty. He acted like the guys my own age.

Eighteen.

Or whatever.

Strat hadn't taken his eyes off me. Hadn't even glanced at my full house. Didn't even look down when he laid his cards on the table. I couldn't move for too many seconds. His look wasn't a look. It was a black hole. All gravity.

I tore myself from his gaze and looked at his cards.

Four deuces.

Fuck.

Losing to deuces was insulting.

Strat leaned back, the coils of his song all over his ripped body. The pot was his, but he didn't reach for it. He just worked me over with his eyes, arm over the back of his chair, knees apart, daring me to search for the bulge in his shorts. I breathed deeply but couldn't get enough air. My lungs had shrunk.

Indy looked at me under the table. "No socks, man. Shit. You're down to not too much."

I was in over my head. Way fucking over. Yet I liked it. More than liked it, I was comfortable when I was out of my depth. All the moving pieces, the inconsistency of the cards, the mess I was making excited and soothed me, a contradiction that translated into *belonging*.

I could fix it. I fixed it every time. My grades were amazing. I was the liaison for the Suffragette Society. I ran the school stage crew like a military operation. It was too easy. If you wanted an omelet, you had to break some eggs.

I'm not saying I chased musicians around after the sun went down because I sat on the edge of my bed and decided to make a mess of my life in order to fix it back up. Insight like that is no more than Monday morning quarterbacking.

I stood and put my hands behind my back, reaching between shoulder blades.

Strat licked his lips, taking his eyes from my crotch and leveling them on mine. I looked right at the motherfucker and pinched my bra hook. He was going to see my tits. The nipples were already hard from his attention. I had pretty good odds on a little damp spot where my panties had been on the pleather.

"Why don't you stop for a minute there?" he said.

I stopped. I didn't have to. Rules were rules. The bra came off. But he was effectively changing them.

Also, I didn't want to take my bra off.

Strat leaned forward a little. A blade of copper hair slid off his shoulder and swung in front of his cheek.

"What?" I asked. "Scared of a little tit?"

"Who are you?" he asked.

"Cinnamon." I flicked my head a little, and my own red hair got out of my eyes. "But you can call me Cin."

"Yeah. No. You got backstage last week from the admin office. I know you didn't fuck Herve Lundren to get there either. Then you and your friend show up places you shouldn't be. The loading dock behind the Wiltern. The thousand-dollar-a-plate dinner at Vilma. And Indiana here fucking stupids right into you."

"Stupid's not a verb, asshole," Indy said.

Strat didn't get distracted. Indy could have broken into the "Star-Spangled Banner" and it wouldn't have snapped the drum of energy between Strat and me.

"Cinnamon's not even a name," Strat added.

"Your mother name you Strat?"

"*Rolling Stone* revealed my name three months ago."

"Stratford Gilliam," I whispered.

He leaned back again, but he didn't spread out. He crossed an ankle over a knee. "Something's up. You have cash. Enough to play with us. No eighteen-year-old has a wad of twenties inside hundreds."

"I'm a fan. I like your music."

"What's your name?"

"You deaf? Cinnamon."

"I can call you Cin."

I touched my nose.

"Tell me your name," he said, "and you can keep the bra on."

He'd read me like a street sign. I didn't want to take that bra off. I wasn't ready for what that would lead to.

Yet I'd wanted to see if I could get out of it.

Dad asked me once why I loved trouble. Why I seemed to enjoy it so much. Why I made my own if I couldn't find it in the wild. I had no answer. Still didn't.

I didn't want it to get out that I was in a hotel suite with Bullets and Blood. If I told this guy my name, I could get into trouble, and not the enjoyable kind.

"Your name." The word *name* was silent on his lips.

My hesitation didn't seem to bother him. He played me at the right tempo, continuing when I thought I'd break and just snap my bra open.

"I've seen enough tits in my time," he said. "But you. Maybe you're a fan, but it's something else. You're different."

Show him your tits.

My fingers twitched on my sides. I was throbbing everywhere. My body wanted him, and my mind was running a four-minute mile in the other direction. I'd lost control of the situation, and as much as I dabbled in trouble, I never lost control of it.

Lock it down. Don't even think your name. Don't even think it. Don't even.

"What's your name?" he asked again.

I swallowed and decided to take off my bra. He'd try to fuck me, and we'd see where that went. I'd fought off men before. My hands crawled to my lower back.

He blinked, and in that split second his jade eyes were hidden from me, I changed course.

"Margaret Drazen," I said, putting my hands on my hips and leaning hard on one foot. "You can call me Margie."

"Nice to meet you, Margie." He lazily picked up the deck of cards. "Your deal."

CHAPTER 2.

Five things about being me.

1) I come from a long line of money. I've got more money in my trust than most people see in a lifetime. I've never worried about having it or getting it. I don't have to work, but I like to. Really like to.
2) I'm connected. If I don't know who I need to know, my father does. I've never had much cause to call in favors or know the right people, except to get into concerts and parties when I was younger. But I can. And knowing that makes all the difference.
3) I grew up quickly. I was born mature. Strat had it right when he said I talked like an old lady. He said that before I was fed shit on sterling silver spoon, then the talk got real and I saw life for what it was. So the politics and backstabbing in law school were child's play. Intra-office bickering is white noise. I win. End.
4) Bullshit makes me really impatient, and drama is bullshit. Drama's never about right and wrong. It's about *feelings*.
5) Feelings are for children. See #3.

CHAPTER 3.

1994

Law offices are snake dens. I learned that at Stanford when I butted up against the old boy network for an internship at Whalen + Mardigian. But I didn't bitch about the partners inviting the guys to a strip club and pulling interns from the group there, because I had the luxury of my own privilege. I felt bad for the women who didn't have my smorgasbord of options, but see… that was a feeling. See Chap. 2 - No.5

So I made clerk at Thoze & Jensen, a multinational firm with twelve offices in the States and an impressive presence overseas. Tokyo. Frankfurt. Dublin. Johannesburg. Hong Kong. But the firm was still as backward as a third-world country. An impenetrable fortress for anyone outside the Harvard/Princeton/Yale Testosterone Mafia, meaning— women. All women, with or without Ivy League degree. We could clerk and we could be associates, but we'd never partner.

We'd see about that.

They hired me as an associate right out of law school but had to clerk me until I passed the bar. Until then, I got a six-figure salary even though I didn't need it.

How?

Easy. I brought them a client.

You thought it was going to be some scandal.

It could have been, but when choosing between sugar and vinegar, it's best to remember vinegar works best as a preservative.

I was a clerk until I passed my bar, and despite what you

may think, I couldn't buy that. Nor did I want to. I rented a house in Culver City and covered it in sticky notes. From the table where I kept my keys, (*Strickland v. Washington. Defines inadequate defense as it relates to result*) to the bathroom mirror (*Ford v. Wainwright. No death penalty for mentally deficient*). Even my car had a note stuck to the windshield (*TORTS – Tarasoff v. Regents. Responsibility of psychiatrist to warn potential victims of harm. Responsibility can be litigated with commensurate award for damages.*)

I didn't have time for men or friends. No one understood me anyway. No one but my family, which was more than enough. I had six sisters and a brother. I was the oldest, and I'm still not telling you my age, or you'll start doing math in your head instead of paying attention.

I was heading for a meeting with the senior partner on a copyright case I'd just been put on, rushing through the waiting room, which was a shortcut to the conference room, with an armload of depositions and pleadings, rattling hearsay exceptions in my head. There were ten categories, and I always forgot one. I walked across past the white leather couches with my folder, feet silent on the grey carpet.

Excited utterances.

Dying declarations.

Declarations against interest.

Present sense impression.

Present state of mind.

Doing good. Almost there…

Prior inconsistencies.

Public records.

Business records exception.

Ancient documents.

And….

And I beat my brain for the last one.

The man pushed himself off a couch as I was looking in my head for the tenth exception instead of out of my eyes for tall guys in suits.

I was midair, shouting, "Family records!" as if getting backed into reminded me that families couldn't be trusted to keep a story straight. The folder I was delivering to the conference room went flying. A shoe fell off. I landed on my butt bone with my legs spread as far as the pencil skirt allowed.

"Oh, shit, I'm so sorry!"

I put my knees together and got back up on my elbows to get a look at the clod who had knocked into me.

He was a god. The kind of guy who could model but didn't because it was too boring. Clean-shaven with brown hair pushed to one side. A bottom lip that had the same fullness as the top. Blue eyes. I had a metaphor for the color tooling around somewhere in the torts and procedures, but it all went blank when he put his hand down to help me up, and I saw a tattoo creep from under his cuff.

I looked at him again.

He looked at me.

"Cinnamon," he said.

"You can call me Cin." The words came automatically, as if coded in my myelin.

I took his hand, and he helped me up. My response might have sounded smooth and mature, as though I wasn't thrown off at all, but it was the opposite. I'd memorized that answer sober, drunk, and dancing. I even said it in my head when someone mentioned the spice. Back when I was a stupid, reckless, wicked girl, it was a calling card.

I got up, not making eye contact with the stares coming from the entire waiting room.

"I'm fine," I said, acting meek. When all the clients returned to staring at their magazines, I turned to the man who had knocked me down. "You going to stand there and let them trample my case file, Indiana McCaffrey?"

I smiled a little, and he smiled back. Wow. Had I been so unconscious when I met him that I'd thought he was only okay-looking? A close second to Stratford Gilliam? Seriously? How had he matured from twenty into this perfectly-chiseled version of a man?

I bent down to get my papers, and he put his hand on my shoulder.

"Let me be the first to get on my knees," he said, crouching before I could respond.

I couldn't believe he remembered me out of the thousands of girls who had thrown themselves at him. I knelt next to him and scooped up papers.

"I go by Drew now," he whispered. "My middle name."

"I go by Margie. My real name."

"I remember."

"I didn't expect you to," I said quietly.

He tilted his head just enough to see me, then he went back to picking up the files. I could see the tiny holes in his ears where he'd let his piercings close up.

"Who could forget you?" he said.

"Oh, please. Flattery only soils the intentions of the flatterer."

"Where's that from?" He tapped the stack on the carpet in an attempt to straighten them.

"My head."

He handed me his stack, and I jammed it into the folder.

"You haven't changed a bit."

I swallowed hard. I didn't have a problem with most of my misspent youth. I'd had fun and finished the job before I completely ruined my life. But I worked in an uptight law firm with a brand made of sedate blues and sharp angles. Former-rock-and-roll-groupie heiress wouldn't look good on them.

"Miss Drazen?"

It was Ernest Thoze standing by the reception desk, senior partner and my boss ten times over. I could have bought and sold him, but that wasn't the transaction I had in mind. I wanted to earn his respect.

I glanced at Drew then back at Thoze. Shit.

Thoze the Doze + Drew the Screw = I-Had-No-Rhyme-

For-How-Much-I-Didn't-Want-That.

Thoze tapped his watch.

"Six minutes," I said. "I got it."

Thoze nodded and paced off. I was always ten minutes early, and fucktard over here had just given me seven minutes of reorganizing to do.

Fucktard smiled like a rock star. I remembered why I couldn't keep my eyes off of him or Strat.

"I knew you were meant for big things," he said.

I turned to face him, getting close enough to hiss. "It's been real fun reminiscing, but let's cut it short. I have a meeting. I'm sorry about Strat. That was fucked up. I wish I could have been there for you, but I didn't know until it was too late."

I didn't wait for a response, because seeing him made me *feel* things. Physical things. Emotions. Perceptions. He made me wonder if my hair looked all right or if my skirt showed enough/too much leg.

I paced off to my meeting, listing all the ways people could tell lies of perception.

Excited utterances.

Dying declarations.

Present sense impression.

He must be a client.

Present state of mind.

Prior inconsistencies.

Gotta be a hundred copyright claims after Strat split.

Declarations against interest.

Business record exception.

Just keep cool and don't give anything away.

Public records.

Ancient documents.

And motherfucking family records.

Boom. I pushed open the glass door to the conference room with finality.

I reorganized all the packets and laid one at each of the six seats with thirty seconds to spare. I opened the blinds that covered the windows looking out into the hall, letting everyone know the room was ready.

Life wasn't like books, not that I had time to read. But in books, there were fake coincidences and chances that changed fake lives. In real life, things happened because you made them that way. I'd never expected to see Indy again because I wasn't looking for him, and when I did see him, I assumed he was a client.

When he walked in ahead of Thoze and four other lawyers, plopped his briefcase down on the visiting lawyer side of the table and smiled at me. My heart sank.

Not a client.

CHAPTER 4.

1982 – Before the night of the Quaalude

It was the era of the deLorean with a car phone the size of a loaf of bread. The era of payphones and beepers. Reagan, *E.T.*, *Rocky III*, poisoned Tylenol, and Love Canal.

I lived all of it and none of it. I looked at the world through a peephole in the front door, outside to inside. Everything was tiny, far away, and in full focus.

My friend Lynn was the lens. She was a card-carrying groupie. She'd gone to Carlton Prep, same as me, and she was, unfortunately, dumb as a box of rocks. The product of two beautiful, stupid people who made a ton of money for being beautiful despite their stupidity.

She was entertaining as hell though. Connected. Older. Fully-sexed. I didn't want to be her, but I knew I had to go through her stage in life. And she needed me because she had a habit of getting her ass in trouble, and I had a habit of creating ways to get her out of it.

The Breakwater Club used to be stuffy and traditional but had changed to a venue for hip Hollywood parties on weekends. They let you smoke anywhere outdoors, but not inside. Which was annoying, especially on March nights when it could get down to fifty degrees by the beach.

Lynn struck a wooden match, hands shaking. She leaned on a concrete planter and cupped her hands over the flame. The corner of her cigarette lit. She sucked hard to pull the cherry. Behind her, the ocean crashed and the sand darkened close to the waterline.

"So fucking annoying," she said. "Like second-hand smoke ever killed anyone."

The guy smoking next to her checked her out with a smart smile. She wore a tube top and a skirt so short that her underwear showed when the wind blew.

I took the lit cigarette from her and pressed the tip to my own, filling my lungs with delicious nicotine. Yoni and Fred were inside.

"Are they both in there?" I asked.

"Yeah. The two of them. The hot ones."

That would be Strat and Indiana. Vocals and guitar, respectively.

And hot, for sure. Lynn and Yoni had been chasing them around for a week. Lynn had taught me so much about how to get through doors. How to ask person A for a favor because they knew person B.

I took it all back. She wasn't dumb as a box of rocks. She was dumb as a box of fox.

"I think tonight's the night," she said softly, leaning into me. She held up three fingers and twisted them around in a bastardization of "fingers crossed." Code for a threesome, which the two boys were famous for and what she had been trying to get herself involved in for a week.

"It's, like, fifty percent more romantic," I said.

She blinked. Didn't get it. I sighed.

"Yoni's in for girl-on-girl," she said. "I'd ask you but—"

"No thanks. Not tonight."

Not yet. I wasn't ready for that kind of thing. I'd done some low-level groping, but nothing close to the intensity of what Lynn chased after.

Yoni poked her head out. Her furry blond bob was held up with a big lace bow, and she wore fingerless, elbow-length gloves with dozens of silver bracelets at the wrist.

"Lynn," she said sotto.

Half the people on the smoking deck turned at the sound, then back to what they were doing.

"What?" Lynn asked.

We stepped to the door, and Yoni came out.

"They have a suite upstairs. Talking about a poker game. You got cash?"

"Yeah," Lynn answered.

"I'm in," I said.

Yoni's gaze sizzled over me, and I realized my error. I was going to be a buzzkilling interloper.

I stamped my cigarette out under my short boot. "Never mind. I'm going to take a walk. See you guys later."

I didn't wait for a response. If Lynn wanted to screw one or both of those guys, I could get a cab home. I didn't go to the street though. I went down the wooden steps to the beach. My feet felt the cold of the sand even through my boots. It had rained earlier in the day, and my steps made half moons of darker sand visible in the floodlights. I walked to the waterline out of reach of the light, not looking back, and sat with my knees to my chest, hugging myself against the cold.

The light disappeared and the night took over a few feet from the line where the sand got flat and wet, streaked with the movement of the tide and punctuated with intestinal piles of seaweed.

I didn't have any feelings one way or the other about the orgy. I wasn't interested. But I liked poker.

I dug my heels in the sand. Fuck this. I didn't know what to do with my body, with my place in the world, with my family. I was trapped in all of it. The water broke, foaming and hissing, a few feet from me. I didn't know if the tide was rising or receding. Didn't matter.

I didn't know what I believed in.

Desperation defined the lives of my friends. They were desperate to fit in, to make their families happy, or to decide who they were immediately. I didn't understand the hunger for approval or validation. The backstabbing and garment-rending over people with dicks made me uncomfortable. Men motivated tears and anguish that seemed unjustifiable. Weird. Out of character. I had friends who were normal one minute then started to have a freaking embolism when their bodies changed.

I felt it too. But we all took the same courses in school. We'd all known it was coming. Why act as if it was a shock?

I'd backed away slowly until I didn't have friends who couldn't cope. No one knew what to do with me. I didn't even know what to do with me. I knew I didn't fit in, and I didn't care. Maybe it was my version of rich girl ennui. Maybe I was just too smart, too good at too many things. Or too acerbic to make those warm girly relationships. I depended on no one. Didn't feel useful.

I felt as though I had more going on in my head than most people, then I thought I was out of my mind for believing that. So I reached out, trying to make more friends. Then I realized how empty relationships were. I realized I really did have more going on in my head than most people, and I started the cycle over.

Lynn had disappeared into the club, on her way to the suite to have a threesome or foursome, and I was left on the beach. I could have made it a fivesome, and why not? What would be the difference either way?

Screwing one or ten people didn't need to be an earth-shatteringly meaningful experience, but I should know why I wanted to besides boredom.

"It's not ennui then," I said to myself.

My face squeezed tight, reacting to having sand thrown in it before my brain fully registered that two shirtless men had run past me, kicking up sand. They dove into the freezing surf.

God damn. Los Angeles was pretty warm in March, all things being equal, but the water was fucking cold.

They swam to the place where the waves rose cleanly and treaded water, looking toward the horizon. When a big one rolled in, curling at the top at just the right moment, they flattened their bodies and rode it in. They got lost in the white froth, then they came up sitting. They high fived. The wave they had ridden continued past them, past the boundary of wet sand, to the dry line six inches from my boots.

Tide was coming in.

One of the men came toward me, pants heavy with water, hair dripping, short beard glistening in the lights of the boardwalk. "Got a towel?"

"No."

"Fucking cold."

"Shoulda thought of that before you went in."

Behind me, the other guy snapped a white hotel towel off the sand and gave it a shake before putting it around his shoulders. He had music tattooed all over his chest. That would be Stratford Gilliam. Unbelievable in person. Even in the dark.

"She's got a point," he said and darted back to the club.

The guy with the ginger beard was Indiana McCaffrey, and he was supposed to be fucking Lynn and Yoni. Instead, he was standing over me, shivering.

"I have fire," I said, handing him my cigarettes and lighter.

He took them and sat next to me. "Thanks." He pulled out two cigarettes, handed me one, and lit both with trembling hands.

"You should probably get inside."

"I like being cold."

"Sure. That's why people move here."

He blew out a stream of smoke. It took a hairpin turn two inches from his lips when the sea breeze sent it behind him.

"You from here?" he asked.

"Los Angeles born and raised. Fermented in Pacific brine and air-dried in the California sun." I flipped my hair so the wind blew it out of my face. He was more beautiful in person than in any magazine. I didn't know how I got to be sitting on the beach with Indiana McCaffrey, but once the cigarette was done, he was probably going to split. Every second counted. "Your Southern accent's mostly gone. You could be a newscaster."

He nodded, or he could have been shivering. "My father didn't like me sounding like a hick, so he beat the accent out of me."

"What else did he beat out of you?"

He glanced at me. "Besides the shit?"

His pupils were dilated eight-balls with blue rings. He was on some sensory-enhancing drug. Quaaludes maybe. Supposedly the blue capsules made you horny and happy enough to melt the awkwardness out of the threesomes. That's what Lynn said. She got blued whenever she could. I kept away from blues. I didn't need to be any hornier or happier.

The top layer of his hair had dried, and it fluttered in the wind as he looked down, rolling the tip of his cigarette against the edge of the sand.

"Shit's the first thing to go," I said.

He smiled, looking up at me with a cutting appreciation. As if I'd touched him in a way I hadn't even tried. Asked him something real. I'd just been fucking around, but I'd hit a nerve, so I didn't shrug it off and ask something different or dismiss the question.

"Came a day," he said, putting the filter to his lips. "Came a day I stopped feeling anything good or bad. He'd beaten that out of me good. I like or don't like things. But everything else?" He flattened his hand and cut the air straight across our eyeline.

"I get it," I said. "I have the same thing. No beatings though."

"Everything's better with a beating."

I laughed, and he laughed with me. For a guy who had no feelings, I kind of liked him.

"I saw you play the KitKat Lounge the other night," I said. "And the party after."

He twisted his body to face me and looked me in the eye. "I knew I'd seen you somewhere."

"I didn't want you to think I was pretending to not know who you were."

"Fair enough."

"But you don't have to stay here to be polite. It's cold."

He shrugged. The shivering had slowed, and his skin had dried. "My friend's upstairs with a couple of girls, and I'm not in the mood tonight."

"I think those girls might be friends of mine."

He turned back to the ocean, mimicking my posture: knees bent, elbows wrapped around the peaks of his legs, shoulders hunched. "You want to go up there, it's room 432."

"I was on the beach to avoid that scene."

"Why's that?"

"Wanted to see if you two idiots would get hypothermia."

He turned to me again, chin at his bicep, hair bending over one dilated blue eye. "How old are you?"

"Eighteen. Why?"

"We're getting a poker game together at midnight. You in?"

I had nowhere to be until morning. And because I didn't give away my hand with my voice or body, I was very good at poker.

"I'm in."

CHAPTER 5.

1994

The copyright case was pretty simple. Bangers, a UK-based pseudo-pop-rap band, had used a few bars of Haydn in their breakout song. Haydn wasn't protected under US copyright, obviously, but Martin Wright was, and he claimed Bangers had used his recording of Opus 33 repeatedly in the song.

Bangers countersued for libel, denying the claims and producing proof that they'd hired a string quartet to play the piece. Martin Wright couldn't prove it was his recording since he claimed they changed the speed so that they wouldn't sync up.

"By way of introduction, everyone, this is Drew McCaffrey," Thoze said.

Drew nodded at everyone, and I thought he lingered on me, but maybe I was mistaken. Maybe I lingered on him.

"Mister McCaffrey is here from the New York office, where he represents the interests of... god, how many musicians?"

"All of them, if I could."

Ellen giggled, sighed, caught herself. She was newly divorced, in her mid-thirties, and suddenly giggling. She was tall and attractive. Well put-together in her daily chignon and Halston suit. Closer to Drew's age and expertise. I had the sudden desire to lick him so I could call him mine.

Thoze continued. "Martin Wright, the cellist, was LA-based at the time of recording, and he's trying to bring this through a favorable court system. Thank you for bringing this to us,

Mister McCaffrey, but no one has a case." Thoze closed his folder. "I say we send Mister Wright on his way."

"They stole it," Drew interjected.

"You can't prove it," Peter Donahugh said, brushing his fingers over his tie to make sure his double-Windsor knot was still where it ought to be. "No one can. The cost to the client would outweigh the award."

Drew put his pen on the table, taking a second of silence to make his case. I'd known a musician puffy from drugs and alcohol. The guy across from me, taking three seconds to get his thoughts together, had the same blue eyes, but he also had a law degree. He still had guitar string calluses on his fingers and a tattoo that crept out from under his left cuff.

The *Rolling Stone* piece I'd read hadn't gone past Indy's devastation over Strat's death. I never heard about Indiana again. Didn't know his career choice post-mortem.

God damn. This suited him.

He pressed his beautiful lips together, leaned forward, and turned his head toward Thoze the Doze. I could see the tendons in his neck and the shadow the acute angle of his jaw cast against it.

I remembered how that neck smelled when I pressed my face against it.

"It was the most popular recording of Opus 33 when the song was mixed." Drew laid his fingertips on the table like a tent. "These guys, Bangers, didn't have a peanut butter jar to piss in. Moxie Zee charged an arm and a leg to produce, but he's a lazy snake. He billed the band for hiring a quartet that never existed, and I know him. He isn't searching out the least-used version of Haydn's Opus."

"A case is only as good as what you can prove," Peter said.

Drew kept his eyes on Thoze when he answered. "He's produced a bunch of paper. Not one actual cellist."

"We're not in the business of proving what isn't there." Thoze wove his hands together in front of him. "Absent something that proves malfeasance, we have nothing."

"What am I supposed to tell Martin? We don't care?"

"Tell him we're looking for something we can act on."

Thoze stood. His assistant stood. Peter and Ellen stood. I took the cue and gathered papers. I looked up at Drew to see if he was going to react at all, and he was reacting.

He was looking at me as if I had an answer. I couldn't move. Ellen tried to linger in the conference room, but in our shared stare and shared history there sat a thousand years, and Ellen didn't have that kind of time.

She cleared her throat. "Margie, can you grab me a coffee from the lounge on the third floor?"

"There's coffee right there," I answered from a few hundred miles away.

"It's better on three."

"I'm going for breakfast," Drew said, not moving. "I'll grab some coffee. Donuts too."

"Send the clerk. That's what they're for."

Was Ellen still talking?

"She can come."

Ellen paused then slinked out.

As soon as the glass door clicked, Drew spoke. "What are you thinking?"

"I'm thinking I had no idea you had a brain in your head."

It really was amazing how his lips were so even, top and bottom. How had I not seen that? Or the way his eyes were darker at the edges than the center?

"Things changed a lot since then."

I was feeling things, and now with his voice sounding like a cracked sidewalk, I knew he was too. That wouldn't do. It made me uncomfortable, as if my skin was the wrong size.

"I'm sorry. About Strat. I know you guys were close."

I'd broken the spell.

Drew pulled his gaze away and put his briefcase on the table, snapping it open when he answered. "Thank you."

"Was it bad?" I had no business asking that, but I had to because I should have been there. I should have done the impossible, leapt time and space, presumed a friendship I might have made up, and been there for them.

"It was bad."

He plopped his briefs in the case. I was supposed to get up and straighten the room out, but I couldn't stop watching him, remembering what he'd been to me for a short time and how those few weeks had changed me.

"What studio did Bangers record in?" I asked.

"Audio City." He slid his case off the table and went for the door.

Just as he touched the handle, I spoke. "Have you done a Request for Production?"

He didn't open the door but turned slightly in my direction, curious and cautious. "I don't see what that would prove."

I stood. "I'm only a clerk."

"I'm sure that's temporary."

I pushed the chairs in, straightening up as I was meant to. I didn't want him to feel pressured to take advice from someone who hadn't even passed her bar yet. Someone who had been no better than a smart-mouthed groupie all those years ago. But I wanted to be heard.

"You want to scare the hell out of them, you call in some favors at Audio City," I said. "Take Teddy out for some drinks. Be seen. And you file a Request for Production to aid discovery. Teddy hands over the masters."

"They'll be mixed down. They're useless."

"There's more to a tape than the music. There's pops and scratches. Match them to Wright's master. It's like a fingerprint."

"That's not true."

"It's true if you believe it is. You're not trying to prove anything. You're trying to get Moxie Zee to crack."

He took his hand off the door handle. I noticed then looked away.

"What you want," I continued, trying to sound casual, "is for your client to be paid for his work, right? I mean, cellists make a living but not that much."

"Not Drazen money."

I ignored the jab. One, he smiled through it. Two, though I

tried to be as anonymous as possible in the office, it was nice to be known.

"No." I pushed the chair he'd sat in under the table. "Not Drazen money. If Moxie Zee is caught lying, most of his artists won't care. Some will think it's cool. But he works for Overland Studios as a music supervisor under his real name. Overland's risk averse. They're not keeping a guy who might have already exposed them to a lawsuit."

"And you think Moxie will pay off Martin under the table over a fingerprinting technique that doesn't exist?"

"People are pretty predictable."

He nodded, bit the left side of his lower lip, tapped the door handle three times, then looked me up and down as if he wanted to eat me with a dick-shaped spoon.

"You're still crazy," he said softly, as if those three words were meant to seduce me.

They did. He was half a room away, and every surface between my legs was on fire. I would have swallowed, but I didn't even have the spit to do it.

"How old are you?" he asked.

"Eighteen."

He walked out, letting the door slowly swing shut behind him, and I watched him stride down the hall in his perfect suit.

Men loved tits, legs, ass, pussy. Men loved long hair and necks. They loved clear skin and full lips. But some men, the right men—men like Drew and Strat—loved cutting themselves on sharp women, and I hadn't been loved for the right reasons in a long, long time.

CHAPTER 6.

1982 – Before the night of the Quaalude

Bullets and Blood was on the verge. *Kentucky Killer* had caught fire and made the small label enough money to keep the lights on. But then the Big Boys went after Bullets and Blood, sending hip-looking A and R guys around with pockets full of promises. They introduced them to music legends like Hawk Bromberg, with his little flavor-saver and sideburns, who talked up his label and everything they'd done for him.

This was background noise in the weeks following, but the morning after I cleaned them both out at poker, I knew nothing. I'd kept my bra on, put my shirt back on, and stretched on the couch for a few hours. Woke up with a headache and a throat that felt like a bag of dry beans.

I had to get to school.

Lynn was gone. So was Yoni. The hotel room looked over the beach and, in the yellow of the rising sun, seemed expensive and luxurious in a different way than the night before.

"Morning," Strat said from the balcony. He leaned on the doorway in a shirt and stonewashed jeans.

Behind him, Hawk smoked a stubby brown cigarette as thick as a middle finger, looking at me as if he was eight and I was a piece of birthday cake. He was a legend, but I wasn't flattered. I was disgusted.

"Where's Indy?" I asked.

"Out for a swim."

Had Strat even slept? He still looked perfect, but maybe my

standards were skewed. He looked as though he partied all the time, and that was what I found attractive about him.

"I gotta go."

"You should come around later."

Hawk nodded, picking the slick brown butt out of his teeth. He sang about heaven and earth with a voice like a fist, but I wasn't loving his real presence.

"Sure." I didn't have time to chitchat. My father was coming back from a business thing in Omaha, and I had to be home.

"Do you have my beeper number?"

"No."

I didn't have time to scrabble around for a pencil and a piece of cleanish paper so I could set off the little black box on Strat's belt. He wouldn't even answer it. He was a rock star.

"Eyebrow," he said. "Six-oh-six E-Y-E-B-R-O-W."

"Six-oh-six? Kentucky? I thought you guys were from Nashville."

"The beeper's from Kentucky."

I didn't move. Just waited for the long version.

"My dad moved to Kentucky. He's a doctor. He upgrades every six months."

Mister Big Rock Star was either too frugal or too busy to get his own damned beeper. Or too much of a kid. Or too attached to his parents.

No matter what angle I looked at that from, no matter how the light hit it, I found it charming.

I had no intention of using that number for anything, though I'd never forget it. My driver was off. So I got a car at the hotel's front desk and sat back for the short ride from Santa Monica to Malibu. It was six thirty in the morning. I had ten minutes to get back.

Nadia, Theresa's nanny, would be up because she didn't sleep. Hector, the groundskeeper, was probably already working. Maria, Graciella, and Gloria. Definitely rousing Carrie, Sheila, and Fiona for school. Dressing them. Making sure homework was done. Deirdre, Leanne, and Theresa would be causing havoc. If I got right in the shower, there was a pretty good chance no one would notice I had even been out.

Except Mom. She was a wild card. She usually slept until eight, but if she drank the night before, she actually woke up earlier. And if she caught me out, she was unpredictable. She'd been pregnant six times since I was born, so she always seemed to be in a constant state of flux. Big. Little. Tired. Energized. Horizontal. Running. One person. Two. She was as likely to lock me out and act as if everything was normal as tell my father, which would be bad. Very bad. All bad. He did not like losing control. He seemed to have two emotions: cold calculation and satisfaction.

I loved him. I loved both of them. But I never knew what to make of them. In the end, I realized they didn't go on and on about how they felt but concerned themselves with actions. I respected that. It was what I thought it meant to be an adult.

I knew I'd pushed it. Playing strip poker with two guys in a semi-famous rock band in a semi-luxurious hotel room? And telling them my name?

My God. I didn't know what my parents would do to me, but everything about it was trouble. Dad cared about what people thought. He cared about appearances and chastity. Even if he wasn't in town, he had the nannies dress us all up and take us to church on Sunday. He made sure we had ashes on our forehead and palm crosses in our hands. He never mentioned God at all, but the Catholic Church always loomed as the ultimate authority.

I'd asked him why, and he said something odd.

He said, "Invisible gods are ineffective."

I had to hope that Strat and Drew had no reason to find out who the Drazens were. How old their money was. They wouldn't. I wasn't anyone to them. I made myself invisible in my mind when the cab got to my house. I gave the cabbie one of Drew's hundreds, ran into the side door, and made it into the bathroom without being seen.

I washed the night away with scalding water.

Six-oh-six eyebrow.

Go over pre-calc in the car.

History

Comp

Stupid's not a verb, asshole.

Forty minutes to memorize a hundred Latin conjugations

Tennis

Photography

Eat something

What's your name?

Catholic Women's Club

Chess Strategy Club

Then?

Then?

Then…

CHAPTER 7.

1994

"I know everything comes pretty easily to me compared," I whispered to Drew/Indiana in the hall before swiveling into my cubicle. I had to pick up my things before doing Ellen's donut run. "But I put some work into being here. I'd appreciate it if you didn't mention we knew each other eleven plus years ago."

"Am I so embarrassing?" He smirked as if he had me over a barrel.

Typical man, thinking it was all about hard work now/today/this week. If word of our history got out, I'd be a slut and he'd be a hero. I'd be fending off advances in the copy room, getting censured for shit I did a decade ago, wondering why I never got the good cases, and he'd fly back to New York and get promoted.

"It's not shame and never was."

"That's my Cinnamon."

"It's Margie now." I spun to face him, my back to my desk and spoke quietly. Terry, the other clerk, was a foot away through the grey half-wall. "Full-time. This is my life. Like I said. I have plenty of privilege but no dick."

"It's 1994."

He said it as if we had entered the modern era and his dick didn't make a damned bit of difference in the workplace. Only a man could think something so utterly incorrect.

He must have seen me boil, because he put a hand up before I could explode. "I'm just giving you a hard time. I never intended to say a word about anything, but I'm in town for the week."

I opened the bottom drawer of my desk and got my purse out. "Fine." I slapped the drawer shut.

"Fine?"

"I have no feelings about it one way or the other."

"Good to see you haven't changed." He winked and slipped out.

CHAPTER 8.

1982 – Before the night of the Quaalude

I didn't have to remember E-Y-E-B-R-O-W or six-oh-six, which I happened to know was a Kentucky number from a friend at Carlton Prep. I got a beep in the middle of chess strategy with a Nashville call back number. An hour later, I was in the passenger seat of a Monte Carlo driving into Pacific Palisades. Strat was behind the wheel, and Indiana was in the back with Lynn and Yoni.

I had no idea why I was there. I wasn't the prettiest girl who hung around them. I hadn't screwed either one of them, though apparently Yoni and Lynn had had a fine time with Strat before the poker game had gotten under way. I didn't understand why I was there because I didn't understand men.

Yet.

It came to me many years later, while reading *Rolling Stone*. During the interview, Indy was sitting in front of a mixing board they'd installed in the Palihood House (He was "producing" because that was always the story arc. Small-town beginnings>cohesion of the group>artistic satisfaction>commercial success>drug use>break up>The Bottom>redemption>rebuilding/branding). His hair was scraggly but intentionally so. His shirt was clean. He'd lost the puff around the eyes, and he was talking about Strat.

"He was like a brother to me, but more. A partner. And when he died, man, it was like someone ripped me open."

In the passenger seat of the Monte Carlo, with the two of them still poker-playing strangers, I didn't know they were like brothers. Years later, reading the *Rolling Stone* article, that Monte Carlo ride came back to me.

I'd been so clueless about how close they were and how lonely they were.

I always assumed I was brought into this world fully formed. Maybe I wasn't. Maybe I didn't understand people the way I thought I did. I chewed on that then forgot it, because it only turned up the heat on a cauldron of stew that had everything and nothing to do with the Bullets and Blood boys.

Indy leaned forward and pointed at a locked gate closing off a road into the foothills of the Palisades. "Up here. Code's fifty-one-fifty." He turned to me, and I could feel his breath on my cheek. "Wait until you see this place."

"It's nice up here," Lynn said before cracking her gum. She was in a black lace corset and tiered skirt. Red, red lips and black, black eyeliner.

"This is the ass-end though," Yoni chimed in. "It's the Palihood."

"Yeah, anything east of the park."

"South."

"East."

I rolled my eyes.

Strat ignored them. "He can't afford it."

"We just got a quarter-million dollar contract." Indy leaned back and kicked Strat's seat.

Strat shook his head. "Have you read it?"

"You don't read Greek either."

Driving up the hill under the clear spring sky, the fact that he'd read the contract and understood it made me look at Strat's arms, his music tattoos, the muscles of his legs, and respect him with a sexual heat.

We pulled up to a house made of glass and overhung with trees and surrounded by tall bushes. When we got out of the car, the shade was a welcome respite from the blasting sun, and the birds cut through the white noise of the freeway.

"It's nice," I said.

"And I can afford it." Indy pointed at Strat as he headed

for the front door.

"Fuck you can," Strat muttered.

Yoni and Lynn had no interest. They'd started bantering about the coyotes in the hills, bouncing with excitement, as we went up the cracked steps onto the pocked flagstones.

"Ye of little faith." Indy opened the door. "I have the down payment next week. Made escrow already."

The black linoleum floors shined, and the sightline went through the house, over the west side, and to the ocean. Yoni and Lynn were already checking out the bean-shaped pool in the back.

You'd think a musician on the cusp of fame wouldn't want to be tied down to a house. He'd want to ride the tour bus and fuck a few hundred girls. That was the norm. But Indy stood in the empty space between the front door and the horizon and lit two cigarettes before handing me one.

"I can move in next week."

"Dude," Strat said.

"Dude," Indy snapped.

Strat turned to me, hands out, pleading. On the whole ride up, I'd wondered why they brought me, and I feared at that moment that they'd gone to the library or talked to their lawyers and found out who I was. Now they were going to ask me for money, and I couldn't give it to them. There was no other reason to put me in that car.

I liked them, but that house had to cost two hundred grand.

Would they threaten to tell Daddy things? The poker? The bra? The smoking? Would they tell him I drank and I kissed? Or that I was a cocktease?

When I brought the cigarette to my lips, my hand was shaking. I didn't know which scenario terrified me most. I inhaled the nicotine and blew out rings as if I had control of this. Whatever this was. It was my first cigarette of the day, and it made my palms tingle.

"Why the fuck am I here?" I asked.

Strat stepped forward, finger pointing at me then Drew.

"Keep me from killing him."

"Fuck you," Indy retorted.

I didn't have anything much more intelligent to offer. "It's a nice house. Needs work. Get an accountant to tell him if he can afford it."

"Let me give you the short version." Strat's comment was directed at me but meant for Indy. "Two fifty minus fifteen percent to WDE. Two twelve and a half. Eighty-three grand. Minus three points to our producer. Two-oh-five. And by the way, we, you and me and Gary—the *band*—we have to recoup *their* points."

"We will. I'm telling you."

"Two-oh-five divided by three? Sixty-eight thousand dollars for a three-year contract. And you haven't even paid your taxes yet."

I rolled my eyes and looked at the ceiling. If Strat and/or Indy noticed me acting my age, they didn't say anything.

"There's income, fucktard." Indy patted his pockets and found a thick marker best suited to sniffing and writing graff. "I need a napkin. Fucking find me a napkin. An envelope. I gotta write on the back of it."

"Fifty grand for the studio we gotta pay back," said Strat the Sensible. "Recoupable. Producer. Recoupable. Equipment rental. Re—"

"Stop it!" I shouted.

I'd had it with the two of them. I didn't know much of anything. I didn't know how to run a business or how to make money, but I knew how to think like a rich person. Maybe that was why they'd brought me.

"You guys. You're so cute with your middle-class shitsense. You act as if it's money to spend. It's not. It's money to make more money. You." I pointed at Strat. "You move in here with Indy. You take your sixty grand, and you set up a studio in the garage or the living room. I don't care where. You." I pointed at Indy. "Get a commercial loan. You lay down the next record here and collect the fifty grand instead of paying it in recoupable expenses. You rent it out to your other musician friends and let them pay your mortgage, and you pay down that fucker because at eighteen percent interest, you're getting killed."

I took a pull on my cigarette. It was so close to the filter that my fingers got hot. Jesus, figuring that out felt good. Whether they did what I said or not, putting it together had been damn near orgasmic. "I need a fucking beer."

CHAPTER 9.

1994

The San Fernando Valley, Van Nuys in particular, was a hell of parking lots and freeway-width avenues. Everything looked new yet coated over in beige dust. Drew and I had split right after the meeting, slipping down the back elevator. It was like the old days when I had a ten o'clock curfew I ignored.

We pulled into the back of Audio City, where the entrance was. Drew put the car into park and leaned back.

"You gonna open the door?" I asked.

"I haven't seen these guys in a long time. Give me a minute to think."

"Get back into your rocker head?"

He smiled, and something about that made me feel really good. "Yeah."

I switched my position so I was kneeling on the seat, facing him. I yanked on his lapel. "Take this off. You look like a fucking lawyer."

"Right. Okay." He wrestled out of his jacket and tossed it in the back. His shirt had light blue stripes and a white collar, and his tie was just skinny enough to be stylish without crossing the line into new wave.

I grabbed it and let it go so it flopped. "Come on, take this off."

He undid it. "I forgot how bossy you are."

"I still can't believe you even remember me."

"You're not forgettable."

"Please," I said. "There were hundreds of girls."

He yanked at the tie, slipping it through the knot. "I was obsessed with you the second you opened your mouth. You scared the fuck out of Strat. He thought he was going to lose me to you."

He leaned his head back on the seat, raising his hand languidly and touching my chin. My eyes fluttered closed, because I'd been too busy to let a man touch me in years, and this man knew how to touch. He ran his finger along the edge of my jaw, down my neck, and I grabbed it before it could move lower.

"We're working."

"What happened to you?" he asked in a whisper.

"I went to law school."

"Before that. You split. We couldn't find you. Strat hung out outside your house. We went to all the clubs. Your friends didn't know where you were."

He didn't know what he was asking. He thought he was going to get some reasonable, sane answer, but there wasn't one.

"It had nothing to do with you," I lied. It had everything to do with him. Every single thing.

"What did it have to do with, Cin?" His voice dripped sex and music, and I wondered if that was just his way of getting back into character.

I reached for his collar and ran my finger under it, revealing the stand of tiny white buttons. "The collar comes off."

"You need to tell me where you went."

"I took a trip."

"We waited, and you never showed up."

He moved his fingertip down my shirt. My breath got short, and I couldn't take my eyes off of his lips.

"Sorry. I flaked. You guys were too intense for me." I didn't know why I had to make it obvious that it was more than that. I could have kept my voice flat and subtext-free, but my inflection got away from me. If he couldn't tell I was hiding something, he was an idiot.

And he wasn't an idiot. That was shit-sure.

"You're not going to tell me, are you?" he said.

"No."

He took his hand away. Relief and disappointment fought for dominance inside me as he flipped his stiff collar up and unbuttoned it.

"We had a good time," he said. "Good coupla months."

"Seven weeks."

"I wasn't even thinking about how long it was going to last. But I was so fucking stupid anyway. Strat was smart. He played at being a reckless musician, but man, he was sharp and fifty years older in his mind. He told me to chill out. He told me the thing we were doing was temporary, and I argued with him like a moron." He shook his head at his stupidity and got the last button undone, snapping the collar away from his neck.

"Looks better," I said, smoothing down the Mandarin.

He took my wrist and sucked me in with the tractor beam of his gaze. "I thought I'd be the one to lose my shit when it ended. But it was him."

I pulled my hand away. I couldn't pretend I didn't care for another second. "What happened?"

"I could ask you the same thing."

"You could."

But he didn't, and I opened the door to end the conversation.

CHAPTER 10.

1982 – After the night of the Quaalude

Rich family. Pig rich. Six nannies, two cooks, and a cleaning staff rich. Multiple estates. We were our own economy. My dad wouldn't experiment with losing a chunk of it for another twenty-plus years.

My father had two brothers, and my mother had a sister she barely spoke to. She'd never said why. She never said much that was worth listening to. She hadn't seemed young to me until the autumn of Bullets and Blood.

This realization happened at a party. We had two hundred people in the house for my parents' anniversary. String quartet. Black tie staff. Open doors to our swimming pool with lotus blossoms and candles floating in it. Attendance was mandatory, so I had to tell Indy and Strat to get their laughs elsewhere.

All the family and business partners were there, all the wives clustered around the couches and most of the men hovering around the bar. Except Aunt Maureen. She never hung around the women. She was my "cool aunt" who ran a business and told the guy she'd been with for the past ten years that she saw no point in getting married. She was talking to my dad and a few guys in suits I knew by sight but not name. I was close by, hanging on every word, when I heard her say something about negotiations with a blue chip company. It was a bunch of numbers and percentages I understood because I remembered everything the adults in my family said about business. But at the end, she laughed.

The sound had a clear, tinkling quality her voice usually lacked. She sounded so young.

Wait. She *was* young.

She was eighteen years older than me. A little less, give or take. And that made my mother fifteen and change when she'd had me.

Over the ice sculpture and through the floral arrangement in the center of the ballroom, I looked at my father and did more math.

I almost laughed at the symmetry of it.

But it wasn't funny. It took me too long to realize what had gone on, but I told myself I wasn't going to be like my mother. I didn't hate her, but I didn't respect her either. She was from a good family. She was beautiful and smart. But she was nothing. She did nothing. Her life was a vacuum that purpose had fallen into, never to be seen again.

I wasn't going to be that, but I was already on the way.

Me in my blue dress and little gold hoop earrings, dressed like a prim little miss. A chiffon-and-silk lie I let them believe. I felt sick.

I was thrown off balance by the impact of a small child. Fiona was five, and she had her arms wrapped around my legs. The others followed. Deirdre and Leanne hugged my legs too. Carrie and Sheila, at nine and eleven, stayed close, looking excited. I was only missing Theresa, who was a year old and had started walking two weeks ago. They looked up at me with eyes in varying shades of blue and green, hair from strawberry-blond to dark brown red. That was what happened when a redhead married a redhead, and my insides curdled like milk on the stove.

"Who's watching you guys?" I was talking about everyone but directed the question at Carrie, the oldest of them and most likely to put together a coherent sentence.

"Everyone's outside. Are you having cake or not?"

How long had I been staring into the middle distance?

Long enough for everyone to move to the garden, leaving a few clustered stragglers by the French doors. I let my little sisters lead me outside, where sibling hierarchy was determined by proximity to the cake. I'd lost any will of my own and hung behind all of them. I didn't really want cake. I'd been sick to my stomach for days, fighting a headache, feeling tender everywhere, but I had a compulsion to act as if dessert mattered.

My mother and father stood behind the cake, smiling for the professional photographer. He wore an *LA Times* press pass. The camera was nowhere near me, but I felt exposed. They'd want a picture with me, and I couldn't. I just couldn't. I could stay relatively anonymous in the world, but people read the pages of news about the Reagan presidency, Beirut, Studio 54 closing, and Hollywood celebrities. After those, but before the stock ticker, came the society page. Weddings. Anniversaries. Deaths of monied men.

My father tapped his glass with a spoon. He was over six feet tall and looked every bit the oligarch he was, with a full head of dark-red hair. My mother was more strawberry, and she held her head high when he was nearby. On that night in particular, she beamed a little brighter.

The guests quieted, and even the photographer put his camera down when Daddy raised his whiskey.

"Ladies and gentlemen," he said, projecting to the back of the room, "thank you for coming. I hope you're all having a good time celebrating this, my anniversary with my beautiful bride."

A chorus of tinkling rose as more spoons met glasses.

A great sound, I thought. *They should try it in the studio.*

My sinuses filled up, and I almost started crying, but my father kissed my mother quickly and went back to his speech.

"We have an announcement!"

Let's hear it, Declan!

Hear! Hear!

"Eileen is about to make me a father for the eighth time!"

"Get off her, for Chrissakes!"

The shout from the back ended in uproarious laughter and cheers from everyone but the children, who didn't understand it.

Except me. But I wasn't a child. Never was, and never would be.

The photographer started snapping again. Dad and Mom indicated we should come behind the table so we could all smile in dot matrix patterns for tomorrow's paper, and I couldn't.

I'd hit my limit. I was going a hundred miles an hour, and the brick wall had appeared inches in front of me, without warning.

I'd taken a pregnancy test that morning. I'd put it away without looking at it and decided I wasn't going to think about it. Not until after the party. Pretending bad things weren't happening wasn't like me, but then again, nothing bad had ever happened to me.

I'd bought it as almost a joke because my period wasn't that regular. But it wasn't funny.

The compulsion to look at the results weighed like a rock in my chest, exploding in slow motion. I had to hide before the shrapnel shredded me from the inside.

My room was a good three-minute expedition across the house, and I took it at a run, slipping on the marble and righting myself. I was crying hard by the time I reached my hallway. Somewhere in the journey, I'd let it go. Everything.

Oh god oh god oh god

I was a sensible person. I knew I had options, and the first step to exploring them was to know what was happening. The nausea and headaches. The tender breasts and belly. The feeling at the root of my hips that something was *happening*. I had to scratch pregnancy off the list so I could move to the next possibility, but I knew I wasn't scratching shit off any list. I just knew.

And when they'd announced Mom was pregnant (again), I couldn't wait another second.

When I got to my room, breathless in my pale blue dress, I slapped open the medicine cabinet where I'd left the little plastic jar. If the liquid was one color, I could forget the whole thing. If there was a brown ring at the bottom—

"Are you all right?"

I spun at the voice in the doorway, leaving my back to the open cabinet. My father stood in the doorway, still thrust forward from his run up the stairs.

"I'm fine," I said.

"Your mother thought you'd take it hard. I told her you were made of steel." His smile was one hundred percent pride.

"I just ate something that didn't agree with me."

I spun and snapped the medicine cabinet door closed, but it bounced back, leaving an inch of the inside exposed. I turned back to my dad, hoping I wasn't disrupting the liquid. Taking the test with eyedroppers and test tubes, I'd felt as if I were in lab class. I didn't want to do it all again. And I didn't want Dad to see it. And I didn't want to be pregnant. And I wanted to rewind the whole thing, so I didn't stupid my way through life.

"You've been so busy with your extracurriculars, your mother is worried." His eyes left mine and went to the medicine cabinet. He wasn't looking in the mirror. They traced the edge, moving up and down.

"I'm a little tired. Can I skip the cake?"

"Be back down in half an hour for pictures."

His sharp expression meant that was an order. I could be green around the gills, and I'd be expected to smile for the camera.

"Okay." I wanted him to go away.

He looked from behind me to my face, scanning it. I felt made of thin blown glass, hollow and transparent. Too fine. Too delicate. Worth too much to be broken without everyone I cared about getting upset over the loss.

I tilted my head down and went around him, to the doorway, where the promised comfort of my bed waited. He'd have to follow me out and leave me alone for thirty minutes. I could do a lot of calming down in half an hour.

I'd just stepped onto the carpet in my room. It was mauve and grey. And by the second step, the colors became a woolen blur as I was pulled back and spun around.

Dad's face was beet red. He held a clear plastic vial in his left hand as he gripped my arm with his right. "What is this?"

"You're hurting me." I tried to squirm away, but he only gripped me tighter.

"What have you done?"

I was so scared I could barely think. My father had never raised a hand to me, but I'd always known there was an ocean of violent potential under his smooth veneer. A cold, deep sea that remained placid but was ever-threatening.

"It's negative!" I shouted, not knowing if that was true. I hadn't gotten a look into the vial before he stepped in.

"This?" He turned the vial toward me, open top to my face.

The yellow liquid had been slipped down. At the bottom, a brown ring of thicker membrane slid down, going elliptical before drooping into a line of accusation.

I didn't have an answer. Not an excuse or reason. Nothing but an explanation of what I'd been doing with my free time, which I was sure he didn't want to hear.

"Who is he?" Dad growled.

Wasn't that the question of the year.

"Let go!"

"Were you raped?"

"What?"

"I'll kill whoever did it."

"Dad! No!" I was crying now. I hadn't had enough time to process what I'd done to myself. I felt the spit and tears as if they were someone else's. Dad's face was lost in a wet, grey cloud, and my breath came in hard sobs. I choked out what I thought was a bit of reassurance. "It wasn't rape."

He twisted me around until I was facedown over my white footboard, the thin wood painful on my abdomen. While I was trying to navigate around that and the tears that flowed with the force of a storm, I felt a sharp pain on my bottom.

A strange clarity cut through my sobs, and my crying stopped as if I'd skidded to a stop at the edge of a cliff while the tears dropped to the bottom.

Dad spanked me again, and the impact turned breaths into grunts. I tried to turn, but he held me and whacked me again. I was confused, pinned. I looked around at him. His hand was raised with fingers flat, and elbow bent to strike me again, and he was looking at his hand as if it had done something he didn't understand.

Then in that split second, he looked down at me, and we made eye contact. He saw me but didn't. I didn't know what he saw. I didn't know what math he was doing in his head. The violent sea within him didn't calm. It didn't drain into a huge funnel and gurgle away, but the tide changed and moved like a lumbering beast, receding over the horizon to a place I couldn't see.

He let me go. I slumped over the footrail. I took two deep breaths, and only the first one was an incomplete hitch.

I had neither choices nor time. My family, for all their money, was very Catholic, very rigid, very traditional. I had tons of privilege but no rights. So if I was going to abort this baby, it was now or never. Let them disown me.

I had to run away.

CHAPTER 11.

1994

Business had been rough for a few years, but Audio City was still the best music studio in Los Angeles. It had a certain something.

Reputation-plus-talent-plus-acoustics-times-equipment-equals-hotter-than-hot.

Before my parents' anniversary party, information like that had mattered to me. But sitting with the head engineer in a soundproof room that smelled of stale sweat and cigarettes, all that mattered was the plan—a ruse to get a settlement—and the client, a cellist who might have been ripped off by a wealthy producer.

"You were the only band in our history who canceled studio dates," Teddy said.

I vaguely remembered him. Back then, before Bullets and Blood, I'd slinked in with Rowdy Boys. Teddy'd had a full head of hair and a smile full of straight white teeth. When I sat in the booth with him and Drew (née Indy), Teddy was made of comb-over and nicotine stains.

"We got our own place," Drew answered.

"Still running from what I hear."

"Yup. Switching over to digital."

Teddy shook his head and snapped a pack of cigarettes off the mixing board. "Fucking digital." He pushed open the pack with his thumb and offered me one.

I took it. Then Drew surprised me by taking out his own pack and lighter.

"It's the future," Drew said, shaking out a smoke.

"Fuck the future." Teddy lit mine then his own.

I pulled on it, tasting the dry heat of tar and letting the nicotine run through my blood. I hadn't smoked in umpteen years, and I'd forgotten how much I liked it.

Teddy picked a little piece of tobacco off the tip of his tongue. "Digital wouldn't help you with your cello problem." He flicked the speck of a leaf away. "It's those pops and hums that make magnetic tape sound warm. It's what got you here. If we recorded on digital, it wouldn't mean shit."

"Yeah," Drew said.

"Digital's gonna kill music."

"Sure."

"But you don't care no more." He flicked his hand at Drew, from his fancy shoes to his conservative haircut. "Lawyer."

"Douche."

Teddy surprised me by laughing. "Yeah. Know thyself, right? I got it. Give me that production request or whatever you call it, and I'll show it to our lawyer. He'll get back to you." He held out his hand to shake Drew's.

Here was the problem. The request for production wasn't worth shit because the fingerprinting thing was made up. Even a shyster lawyer would figure that out.

"How about a deal?" I said.

Teddy's hand froze midway up, and he looked at me. Drew looked both surprised and curious.

I swallowed hard. "Let us down into the master archives for a Bullets and Blood record. The debut was recorded here, right?"

"Right."

"We'll just peek at the Opus 33 masters. See if it's worthwhile so you don't have to blow two hundred an hour on a lawyer. In return, Indy here will show you how they're going digital. Show you the right equipment. So you can decide for yourself if you can switch."

Teddy stubbed his cigarette into a half-full ashtray. I

glanced at Drew. His head was tilted down and toward me, thumb to forehead to hide his expression. His cigarette burned hot to the filter as he smiled.

"Yeah," Drew said, looking up. "We'll do a consult. Above board. You can probably go digital without switching completely. I know you get people and lose people because you're analog. Let's see if you can't do both."

Teddy considered, looking away, then back at us. Shifting his box of smokes, shaking his foot, then nodding to himself.

"Yeah, why the fuck not?" He stuck his hand out again, and Drew grabbed it. "Why the fuck not?"

CHAPTER 12.

1982 – Before the night of the Quaalude

They started getting that studio together almost immediately. They had recording and tour dates to keep. So during the day, the house was filled with workmen, artists, and sound engineers in leather Members Only jackets.

I was confused about Strat and Indy. For the next week or so, I was with them all the freaking time. Like a piece of furniture for the new house. Sometimes they beeped me, and sometimes I E-Y-E-B-R-O-Wed them. I met them wherever they were, and we proceeded to act as though we were all in some kind of relationship.

But they didn't make a move. Strat had eyes like fingers—they had a way of getting between my skin and my clothes. But he never did anything about it. Not in the week after I told them how to have their house and live in it too.

Once, when we were at a party in Malibu, Indy put his hand on my shoulder and said something in my ear. I don't even remember what it was, but the music was loud, so he had to talk in my ear if he wanted me to hear him.

Strat came up right after that, like a hawk, and put his finger in Indy's face, lips tense. Indy shrugged. It was the first time I saw them act like anything but best brothers.

Indy put up his right hand. "Pledge, asshole."

"Fuck you." But Strat put up his right hand. I could see the matching snake tattoos inside their forearms. "Pledge open."

"Nothing," Indy spat. "Nothing, okay?"

"Closed, dude. I'm sorry."

They put their hands down and hugged, back-slapping as if they'd had a whole conversation.

"What was that about?" I asked when Strat drifted off.

Indy shrugged, and someone came to talk to him. Male-musician-slash-producer-slash-A and R guy. Thirties. Black plastic sunglasses with red lenses hiding his blued-out dilated pupils. Cartoonishly hip. Guys like that were always talking to Strat and Indy, and they had a way of making sure I was treated like a life support system for a pussy. It would take three minutes for him to angle his body so that he was between Indy and me, then he'd turn his back to me.

Like clockwork, I was looking at the back of his jacket.

Fuck this. I didn't understand any of it. I went inside, picking my way through couplings and conversations on my way to the front door. I'd opened it, letting the cool West Side breeze in when Strat caught up.

"Where you going?" he asked, nipples hard from the night air.

I let my hand slip from the doorknob. "To buy you a shirt."

He gave me that look. The one that made me warm and tingly. The room was full of women wearing strings and little triangles, yet he was looking at me as if he wanted to devour me skin to bone.

Yes, it turned me on, but it also annoyed me.

"What was that about back there? With Indy?" I asked.

"What was what?"

"Fuck this."

I opened the door, but I didn't get far. He leaned over and pressed it closed.

"You don't know?" he asked. "You can't tell?"

"Since the first day you brought me to this house, you've treated me like a little sister—"

I had more to say. Much more. A speech worthy of Ronald Reagan, but he laughed. I just ate those words, chewed and swallowed them, because I'd seriously misread something. He opened the door, still smiling like a fuckhead.

"Beep us," was all he got to say before I left.

I had an orange button on my beeper. I pressed it, and my driver pulled up. Like magic. His job was to take me to and from whatever activity I had going on. His job wasn't to tell me where to go or tell my family where I was. I barely made it half a block back toward home before I knew I'd beep six-oh-six E-Y-E-B-R-O-W. Or Indy. It didn't matter. I was addicted to them the way Lynn was addicted to blues. The excitement of their company was the best drug in the world.

CHAPTER 13.

Here's a comprehensive list of what it means to be mature for your age.

1) You see people through their lens, not yours. So there's less getting offended. Less reactive bullshit.
2) You have perspective but not experience. You know it all shakes out in the end. So small problems are small, and big problems are small.
3) You get cocky because you're mature and you know it. Stupid mistakes are other people's problems.
4) Your body is still a slave to your brain, and if your brain is thinking about grown-up shit, like sex, your body is going to be a hotbed. And if your body matures early... well, follow the yellow brick road. The Emerald City has its legs spread for you.

CHAPTER 14.

1982 – Before the night of the Quaalude

The house in the Palihood had a thousand square feet of unpermitted add-ons. Some even made sense. Most didn't. One bedroom was five feet wide and had outdoor wood siding on one wall. One add-on was only accessible via five treacherous two-foot-high steps to an attic the shape of an inverted V, and another bedroom was only accessible from the outside patio and through a closet.

I arrived one afternoon after a respectable activity I could never recall in black pumps and a Chanel jacket. The house was dead except for the open door and obscure punk playing from the sound system the boys had installed over the lead-painted walls and chipped molding.

I didn't announce myself. I never did. I was a piece of furniture, more or less. I heard voices from one of the spare rooms. I passed through the third bathroom, into the closet, and almost opened the louvered door to reveal the sound when I stopped. A cry had come from the other side of the door.

The louvers gave me a choppy view, but I saw enough skin to make me take a step back. I heard panting. Groaning. A man's voice. Strat. I took a second step back. Stopped. The doors had a space between them, and I leaned forward and looked.

I recognized the girl from her silky brown hair. When she moved, it swayed over her shoulders. She was on her hands and knees. Strat was behind her, fucking her so hard my face flushed and my body's heat level went deep in the red. I could smell them. Their sweat and something funkier. The scent between my legs plus a man. I touched the wall. I needed it to hold me up.

Leave. Turn around.

"Take it, baby," Strat muttered, hands gripping her ass. His skin was satin with sweat.

I wanted him. I wished I was the girl with the brown hair, taking it. I shifted a little so I could see the place where their bodies met. His cock sliding in and out of her.

God god god I want it.

I was blocking the way, but I didn't want to go back and I couldn't go forward. All I could was hope that no one wanted to go into the spare bedroom right then. I shifted, nervous someone else was near me.

The second woman had curly blond hair and generous naked hips. I wished I was her, naked with them. Laughing about some whispered words.

You're nuts. This is so past what you're ready for.

"You want to eat her out, baby?"

"Yes," said Straight Brown Hair. She turned to Luscious Hips, still getting fucked, and her eyes lingered on the louvers for a moment.

She saw.

"Let me kiss your pussy."

No. She didn't.

Luscious Hips sat right in front of Brown Hair and spread her legs. I didn't think my clit could have been more engorged or my pussy wetter. I was glued to the scene as she laid her face between her friend's legs. I couldn't see what she was doing, but Strat, that voice…

"Eat her hard. Suck on it. *Mmf.* Yes. Make her come."

"I'm so wet. So wet," Luscious Hips shouted.

Strat put his hand between mouth and cunt. I didn't know what he was doing, but the intersection of those three things aroused me so much. I did the unthinkable. I stuck my hand under my skirt and tore my panty hose open to get under my cotton briefs.

I nearly collapsed at my own touch.

"Get it wet," Strat commanded as the girl on her hands and knees sucked his finger. "It's going in your ass."

Did he say that?

I think I'm going to die.

The girl who was getting fucked had her face in Luscious's pussy as Strat stuck one finger in Fucked Girl's ass.

"Yes!" she looked up long enough to affirm.

Strat put in two fingers. She shouted, face planted in pussy. Luscious had Fucked by the back of the head, pushing her mouth into her cunt, pumping her hips across Fucked's face while Strat pumped away and got three fingers into her ass.

Oh god, I want that I want that.

But I didn't want to come. I pinched my clit to shut it up. I had more to see.

Luscious came, crying, "Eat my pussy eat me god yes baby yes eat me." She groaned and threw her head back in relief.

God, that was hot. I wanted someone to eat me out.

Strat held out his hand and said something to Luscious. She reached into the night table and pulled out a bottle of baby oil.

What are you doing, Stratford?

He poured it on Fucked. Down her back and in the crack of her ass. Then he massaged it inside.

"You ready?" he said, handing the bottle back to Luscious.

"Fuck me in the ass."

I swore the backs of my thighs tingled, and every nerve ending between my legs nearly exploded.

He pulled his dick out of her and moved it up between her ass cheeks.

He's going to do it.

Fucked's face tightened and she grimaced, eyes shut, teeth grinding, as Strat slowly but purposefully put his dick in her ass.

"How you doing, baby?" he asked.

"All the way," she said. "Take my ass."

I watched his dick disappear in her asshole, and I squeaked.

They didn't hear me.

I thought they didn't.

Luscious put her hand between Fucked's legs.

I didn't see the rest. I heard the squeaking bed, the shouts and moans, Strat barking when he came in her ass. My eyes were closed as I stroked myself to the most explosive climax of my young life.

As soon as it was done and the three of them were laughing and panting, I pulled my hand out of my panty hose. A line of pussy juice stretched between my second and third finger. I curled them into a fist and backed out of the closet.

Strat was right. I couldn't handle him.

CHAPTER 15.

1994

"Aa-*choo*." I was on my fourth or fifth sneeze.

Audio City kept a rust-painted trailer-slash-shipping container in the north corner of the back parking lot. Teddy had given us the padlock key, and when we opened the back doors, we found a wall of banker boxes stacked to the ceiling. They were ordered by date, with the older shit deeper in the back, except when they weren't. We had to look at every box and hope that the label was correct. We found Martin Wright's Opus 33 sampler master box pretty quickly, about a third of the way through. It was labeled with his name and the year. Drew put it on a low pile and wiggled off the top. The box had become misshapen from dampness. The smell of mildew got sharper with every pile we unearthed.

Contracts. Invoices. Master tapes. A pencil case.

"That's weird," I said.

Drew handed it over. Shiny orange vinyl marked with pen. I pulled the zipper open. It was empty inside but dusted with fine white powder. I held it open for Drew.

When he looked, he laughed. "Of course. We could probably open up all these boxes and sell coke out of the back of this container."

I zipped it closed and tossed it back in the box. "He's a cellist. I can't even imagine what the rest of these have in them. We taking the whole thing?"

"More likely than not." He jiggled the top back on.

We'd found what we came for, but we were both hesitating.

He looked toward the back, where another ten feet of solid banker box stood. A thick wall of musical history.

"You're thinking what I'm thinking," I said flatly. The container was hot and oppressive, yet I didn't want to leave it. "We did come for the *Kentucky Killer* masters."

"You have to get back to the office."

"More likely than not."

"You can't stay here with me. Already you've been with the visiting attorney too long."

"And a law clerk can't call in sick for the rest of the day or anything."

"You'd have to make it up over the weekend." He put his hands on a high box and slid it down, then he put it in my outstretched arms. It said "Neil Young – 1990."

"Yeah. I hate working weekends." I put the box with the rest of the early nineties. "Maybe five minutes. Then I'll grab a taxi back to the office."

"You should run into the office and call. I don't want you to get in trouble on my account."

He had dust on the shoulders of his shirt, and he'd rolled up his sleeves, exposing the tattoos on his inner arms. I'd done a good job stripping the lawyer costume.

"Five minutes." I held out my arms for another box. "Ten. Honestly, I already told Dozer traffic might keep me here. And I have a family dinner tonight. So they don't expect me until tomorrow."

"Saturday."

"Come on, you know the drill. Six days a week, et cetera."

He slid another box off the top. I'd never heard of the artist. He put it gently in my arms, still holding it. "I'm glad you got your shit together."

"You too." I whispered it because I wasn't just returning a nicety. I was speaking a deep truth.

Seeing him again wasn't just a happy coincidence. He scared the shit out of me. I didn't do feelings. They didn't rule me. I did what I wanted, when I wanted, how I wanted. But I was scared, and fear made me uncomfortable.

I decided discomfort was all right though. I wanted to be around him.

His fingers grasped my elbows while he held the weight of the box. "I'm not together. I just have a law degree."

He wanted to tell me something, and I wanted to tell him something. We couldn't. We were different. We didn't know each other and we never had, but the pull was there. I wanted him to know me. I wanted to tell him my secrets. Not because of who we'd been, but because something about his puzzle pieces fit my puzzle pieces. I felt a clicking, like the snap of one piece into another.

I stepped back with the box, and his fingers brushed my arm as I pulled away.

That felt nice.

I turned away and put the box on the pile. Fear was uncomfortable, but the rainstorm between my legs wasn't much better.

CHAPTER 16.

1982 – Before the night of the Quaalude

I happened to know that most stars, real stars, didn't get mortgages. They paid cash or had their corporations loan them the money, so they paid interest to themselves. But Drew and Strat, and Gary to a lesser degree, were normal guys on the brink of becoming real rock celebrities.

We lived on chips and pretzel rods because we were young and skinny. Indy lounged on the blue velvet couch, plucking on his guitar, and Strat scratched his head over the papers laid out over the coffee table. I had my legs slung over the arm of a matching blue velvet chair.

"Can you start booking the studio in August?" I asked.

Indy strummed his twelve-string. Even without an amp, the sound was thicker than a six-string, and he got his fingers into the narrow spaces between them as if he'd been playing since he was seven.

"Yup," Strat said.

He didn't have a shirt on, and I tried not to look at him. Strat was so beautiful it hurt. The promise of sex had diminished since poker night. Part of me said to hell with them, and the other part just wanted to know why.

Indy, Gary, and Strat were tight. Real tight. They'd grown up together in Nashville. Only sons in their families. Graduated from their local suburban high school. Like cupcakes dropping out of the same pan. Different, but all from the same batter.

An empty pack of Marlboro Reds landed in my lap.

"We're out," Strat said.

"There's a carton in the fridge," I said.

His knees bounced, and the swirls of musical staffs buckled where his body folded. A snake coiled around his firearm, biting inside his wrist. Gary and Indy had the same snake tattoo. Gary had married young and fathered up quick, so he wasn't around unless there was music to be made.

"Tell me what that snake's about," I said. I wanted to get him a box of smokes, but I didn't want to do it because he'd told me to. He was a bossy jerk. Sexy and powerful, but jerky.

"It's about you getting a fresh pack."

I didn't move. Indy ran his pick over his twelve strings. I didn't think he was paying attention.

"You all got matching tattoos so you could be a fucking asshole? Shit, I can get one too."

"Why? When you're a bitch already?" Strat's words and tone didn't match. The words were cruel and divisive. The tone was warm and friendly. His face invited me to kiss it, as if he was the only one who would tolerate Margie-the-bitch instead of Cinnamon-the-groupie.

It took me a split second to put together a snappy retort, but Indy cut it off by putting down his guitar and standing. He shot Strat a dirty look and paced out of the room. Strat watched him.

Something was going on, and Strat was too cool a customer to tell me.

I bounced off the chair and followed the guitarist. The house was barely furnished or painted. The guys didn't have the money or time to do the fancy stuff. They had parties, but everyone sat on the floor and in folding chairs. I crossed to the south side of the house where I could see the pool. They'd had that cleaned and finished because to have a party, you needed a pool.

The kitchen had nothing of use in it. Paper plates and plastic forks. The gas was hooked up but was used to light cigarettes and heat spoons of white powder. The fridge had beer, vodka, cigarettes, and a china tea saucer with blue pills arranged around the center circle.

Indy stood in front of the fridge, pulling out a carton. He flipped his wrist, and the box spun midair, dropping on the island counter with a *slap*. Red-and-white packs swirled out. I grabbed one before it fell off.

"It's not your job to do what he tells you," I said.

"Can I ask you a question?" He took a pack for himself and cracked the plastic, letting it flutter to the floor without a second look. Both of them were fucking slobs.

"Sure."

"What do you want?"

"Life, liberty, and the pursuit of happiness?"

He didn't respond, verbally or otherwise. He just wedged out two cigarettes and held the pack to me. I took one.

"Stop the bullshit. You're past that." He took a zippo from his pocket and clacked it open. "*We're* past that."

He lit me. I blew out a stream as he tilted his head to light his own, cupping it as if we were in a hurricane instead of a kitchen. He was unselfconscious in that second, and I admired his face and shoulders.

"Be more specific then," I said.

He clattered a glass ashtray between us. "You don't wonder what's going on here?" He pointed his finger down and made a circle.

Here. I knew exactly what he was talking about, yet he was so vague I could have kept the game going on long enough for Strat to stroll in for his smokes. But I couldn't. I was as tired of this shit as he was. Both. Neither. All. None. The space between them was getting uncomfortably tight.

"You mean that you guys are always beeping me, and you keep me around but no one's fucking me?" I ask.

"There you go."

"Yeah. I wonder that."

I wondered it at night, when I was home alone with my hands under the sheets. When I felt inside myself, the edge of the unbroken membrane tight on my finger. When I imagined some composite of the two of them was on top of me. Or one or the other. Or they fought over me, and both won. I didn't know what or who I wanted, but my body got wet for both Sexy Strat and Sincere Indy. Not that I knew what to do about it. I was old for my age, but there was nothing like actual experience.

"Little Stratford and I, we don't fight over women."

"Okay."

"That's the deal."

"You're implying you're fighting over me," I said.

"Yeah."

"You know what that does for a girl's ego, right?"

I didn't actually believe him. That was the problem. I was cute as hell, but come on.

"When I needed Strat, he was there for me. My father was a drunk fuck." Indy rolled the ashes off the tip onto the amber glass of the ashtray. "Still is. I needed this house for a reason. The guest house in the back? It's for my mother. To get her out of there. So when I finally talk her into leaving him, she has somewhere to go where she feels safe. If I'm hotel to hotel on a bus, that's great, but it's like leaving her to rot. And the guy in there"—Indy jerked his thumb toward the living room, where his best friend was probably still looking over paperwork—"he gets it. I can't do any of this business shit without him. My head's not in it. He's giving up a chunk of his advance to make this house and studio happen."

"I'm glad, Indiana. Really. He's a great friend." I stamped out my cigarette. "What do you want out of me?"

His frustration was bigger than anything we said. His fingers curled, and his teeth gritted. He stepped forward and put his hands just under my chin, an inch from touching them, as if it was as close as he could get. As if his palms and my jaw were the north sides of two magnets.

"I'm fucking nuts about you," he growled, then leaned down, so his face was level with mine. He smelled like tobacco and cologne, with a hint of music and risk. How many times had I watched his fingers on a guitar and wished they were on me? "You have to make a move," he said more softly but with urgency. "You have to choose."

"You're not supposed to have feelings." I said it as if "supposed to" mattered at all.

Strat's voice came from the patio. "Dude." He took the length of the kitchen in three steps, snapped up a pack of cigarettes, then pointed at Indy with the same hand. "Watch it."

"Is he telling the truth?" I asked. "You have a deal about me?"

"A deal?" Strat asked, ripping the plastic off his pack. "I wouldn't call it a deal."

"What do you call it?" Indy asked. "A pledge?"

"Call it a fucking truce."

"You guys are both…"

Insane.

Annoying.

Beautiful.

Looking from one to the other, knowing I could have either, I couldn't pick an adjective, much less a man.

I'd never liked feelings, even before I consciously pushed them away. They made me feel like seven people living in the same skin. Now I had these two guys looking at me as if I was supposed to say something.

What did they want out of me?

One or the other?

What was normal about this? I hadn't kissed either one of them.

Or anyone.

I threw my hands up. "Fuck you both."

I walked out. I didn't want the car to get me. I wanted to walk this off. This bullshit. This pressure. I couldn't admit I was in over my head. I'd never admit a situation existed that I couldn't handle, especially not something as basic as two guys wanting me to choose between them.

I was warmed by the setting sun, but the air chilled my skin. Good. I wanted sensory distraction. Anything to make this shit run in the straight line.

What did you expect?

Nothing. I hadn't expected anything.

No, I'd expected them to choose. I'd suspected that one of them liked me, and the other one kept me around as a courtesy to the other, and I expected that the one who liked me was Indy. And that brought about the bigger question.

Which one did I want?

Both. Neither. Either. Some fourth choice.

"Hold up!"

I thought about not turning around. Just walking to the nearest cross street and calling the driver. I got three steps while deciding what to do. I heard the footsteps quicken behind me, and I turned to see Strat. He was wearing the jacket he kept by the door.

"You got dressed. Nice going."

"Hold up," he repeated, grabbing my elbow.

I yanked away. "You guys need to work it out and get back to me."

"No, baby. You need to wake up. That guy back there? You're not going to find anyone better in your life. You turn your back on him, and you're an idiot."

I was surprised. Here he was, the god of them all, lean and sharp with a voice like a fallen angel, advocating for his friend.

"Why do I feel like a pawn in some game you guys got going?" I asked.

"It's not a game."

"What if I want you?" I didn't mean to say I wanted him, even though I did. I didn't mean to imply I'd made a choice because I hadn't even known there was a choice to be made.

"Sorry," he said, narrowing one eye and shaking his head slightly. "I'm not that kinda guy." He started to walk away.

"I saw you," I called, and he stopped. "With two girls. Couple of days ago."

"Yeah?" He tilted his chin up as if I could swing at it if I wanted, he didn't care.

"It was hot."

"That shit's not for you, Cin. That's a couple of blues and

boredom. Not your scene."

"How do you know?"

"You're too good for that shit. He's too good. This is fucked up, the whole thing. I don't know who you are or what planet you're from, but it's not mine. It's his." Without another word, he walked back up the hill, long hair flipping as he stepped into the wind.

I watched him turn into the gate, then I hit the little orange button on my beeper. If I went right home to change, I could make it to the Suffragette Society planning committee. I needed to get away from this weird fucking scene.

CHAPTER 17.

1994

I'd stopped sneezing. Either we had gotten so deep into the trailer we hit ancient allergens I didn't react to, or my body just gave up.

Drew's arms and shirt front were covered with dust, and he had a war-paint-shaped grey streak across his jaw. It was getting late and his cheeks were getting a dark shadow. I felt as if we were no closer to the box for Bullets and Blood, and I was close to giving up. But every time I thought to mention it, I stopped myself. I enjoyed Drew. His connection to my life before. The pain we shared. Even the shared pain he didn't know about.

"I kept the business going, even after the band broke up," he said. "Gary wanted to find another lead, but I was done. I just wanted that house." He picked up a box. Looked at the label. The handwriting had changed an hour earlier. Someone must have gotten another job.

"Did your mom ever move in?"

"Yeah. After my dad died of liver failure."

I took the box from him. *Rick Springfield.* "Fuck him then."

Drew laughed. "Yeah. Fuck him."

I laid Rick's box on top of the others. We'd developed a quick system so we could get all the boxes back in place, but it would still be a big job. We were deep into the woods.

I went back in to meet him. I was going to say something like, "Hey, I think we gotta ditch this," but he stood over an open box, looking at the contents with silent reverence, and I knew. I stood next to him. It was late, and the trailer's fluorescents flickered blue.

"Is this it?" I said, standing next to him, staring at the box's contents.

Master tape boxes. Ampex. Four of them. A folder. An envelope. He put his hand on a box marked *Kentucky Killer.* They'd recorded it for Untitled Records at Audio City before I came into the picture.

"Nothing happened," he said, more to himself than me. "When we did this, we could have been anyone. But nothing happened."

"You're not the first."

"Remember his voice? The way he grumbled then sounded clear in one breath? He developed that here. Before that, he sounded like a girl all the time. See, he could imitate any voice perfectly. Any accent. He could repeat Russian back to a Russian perfectly and not understand a word of it. But he didn't want to sound like anyone else. So he was trying to create this new sound during that first session, and he sucked. So bad. All over the place. And we were so fucking high. Really high. Everything sounded like shit. The studio smelled like pot and donuts."

He took a break to smile into nothing. He was beautiful. Radiant.

"What changed?" I asked.

His eyes moved toward me, and the answer was in his intensity.

"After you left?"

"His voice. What changed his voice?"

"We were laughing at Gary. He was doing an imitation of his kid. She was two and said pickups instead of hiccups and fillops instead of flip flops. And..."

A smile spread across his face. He pinched the top of his nose between his thumb and first knuckle.

"Strat couldn't breathe. We thought he was still laughing but he was choking on a fucking donut." He took his hands away and looked at the ceiling. "Oh my God, what happened?

I remember. I gave him the Heimlich. He spit up this wad of donut that looked like an oyster. We're laughing. I nearly broke his ribs and we were laughing. But his voice…his esophagus must have gotten shredded or something. Or his throat felt different and knew how to do it. He had a way of hearing that went right to his lungs. He did it once and never forgot it. Fucking gift."

He tilted his head back to the box and slid out a set of reels.

"You miss him. I'm sorry."

"I wish I could have stopped him."

I didn't expect him to put his arm around me, but he slid it over my back, up my spine, and over my shoulder, then he pulled me to him. I watched as he took the top off the smaller box. Inside was a clear plastic reel with brown magnetic tape. It didn't look magical, but to him it was, and we stood in silence for a minute as if praying to it. Then he put the top back on as if shutting out a thought.

His arm tightened around me until I had to loop my arm around his waist. From there, the rest was a dance. He turned. I turned with him. He bent down. I leaned up.

He smelled different. He was cologne and tweed. Sharp and clean.

I turned my head before our lips met, and though that movement came with the knowledge that I didn't know this man, I considered telling him what had happened to me.

CHAPTER 18.

1982 – After the night of the Quaalude

I didn't know what to pack, but I knew I had to go. I yanked my smallest Louis Vuitton suitcase from the back of my closet and slapped it open. I didn't know what to put in it, so it was first-grabbed-first-served.

Outside, the anniversary party was breaking up. Long black cars headed down the drive, just moving dots of white and red lights. I didn't have much time.

I had to get out of there.

Out of that house and to an abortion clinic. I'd come to terms with being disowned. I wasn't having this baby. Not now. Not scared in my room with a party going on downstairs. Not with my mother getting a hundred congratulations for being just as pregnant as I was. Not with the spanking I'd just gotten still stinging my ass.

He'd never done that before. Would he do it again?

I picked up the phone to beep… who? Lynn or Indy or even Strat, who was the last guy I'd beep unless I was desperate.

Which I was.

Desperate.

Time was slipping away, and the consequences of my stupidity were going to land like an anvil in a cartoon. I'd be flat. I didn't know what my parents were going to do, didn't know if my father had even had a chance to tell Mom anything. But I couldn't get the last half hour back. I'd spent it staring out the window, trying to sort my head out. Identifying feelings for what they were. Useless.

This is fear.

Ignore it.

This is shame.

Pat it on the head and send it away.

This is regret.

Kick it.

I tapped the headset on my upper lip. Lynn's family knew my family. All my friends were from the same circle. I'd be sent right back home.

E-Y-E-B-R-O-W

I dialed so fast my fingers slipped on the buttons, and I had to start over. *Ring. Ring.* Three beeps.

I put in my number. They wouldn't know it. I'd always called from the car phone or a phone booth. Never from home. They didn't know where I lived. Smartest thing I ever did on one hand, because it protected them. On the other hand, when the beep came through, he wouldn't know who it was from.

So I waited.

When the phone rang, I picked it up in a rush. "Strat?"

He was outdoors. I heard traffic whoosh and the sound of music far away. A party? A show?

"Cin? What's up?"

His voice was rock candy, sweet and rough, making a beeline to the part of my brain that didn't do any of the good thinking. He must have caught the remnants of panic in my voice, because he didn't sound like his usual casual self. And what was up? What could I tell him over the phone from my own house?

"I need you to meet me at Santa Monica and Vine at midnight. At the gas station."

"What's wrong, baby?"

"Don't call me that." As I was finishing my sentence, the doorknob to my room turned.

"What—?"

I hung up before I heard the rest of the question.

CHAPTER 19.

1982 – The night of the Quaalude

Palihood wasn't even a word before my friends got snobby about the wrong side of Pacific Palisades. But it took Palihood House a week and a half to get a reputation, which Strat shrewdly made work in their favor.

Sound Brothers Studios. They trademarked it on a Tuesday and filed corporation papers by Friday. The sound boards weren't even set up yet, and they were already stealing business from Audio City.

Their parties were riddled with musicians. Some were at the height of their careers. They expected blowjobs. Hawk Bromberg could scream over classical guitar, which qualified him to get his dick wet within minutes of arrival. It was an entitlement, and that night, he got a look at me in my cutoff shorts and Marlboro miasma and decided he was entitled to me.

I clapped the heel of my denim wedge against the shag carpet and listened to him talk to me as if I wanted to fuck him. I didn't want to fuck him. I wanted Indy and Strat. I had the keen and unpleasant sense I'd lost them both by not choosing.

Hawk was telling me something about how record execs are all assholes and sellouts. Those cats weren't artists. They didn't understand the process (man) and those dudes are about money and not the music (man). Did I dig?

I did dig. His eyes were wet and his lips were dry, and I could dig it. I was as relaxed and happy as I ever got. Tiptoeing through fucking tulips.

"They got a bathroom in this place?" he asked.

"Yeah, sure. I'll show you."

I was like the lady of the house, even though I wasn't screwing either of the men who lived there. I was polite, I kept my pants on, and I kept my blood alcohol level low. I got to be in love with both of them without having to choose between them.

I wove through the crowd, Hawk behind me with his hand on my back, which I thought nothing of. He just didn't want to get separated. Indy saw me through the crowd, out of the corner of his eye while talking to Willie Sharp. Lynn winked at me when I passed her. We had to stop a few times to say hi to this one or that, but I was mindful of Hawk's needs and pulled away quickly to reach the quiet part of the house. Strat was in the kitchen, sitting on the counter with his feet on the island while two girls giggled at his side. One had her hand on his leg.

I told myself I wasn't jealous because jealous was a feeling—and I didn't have those. Also, Stratford Gilliam wasn't mine to get jealous over. That had been established.

The line for the bathroom was down the hall. I would have told him to just go pee in the bushes like all the other guys, but he'd said bathroom, not bushes. Maybe he had to do a sit-down session. Maybe he had a phobia.

"I'll take you to the bedroom suite," I said.

You're rolling your eyes.

I'm rolling my eyes too.

There are some mistakes you only make once because the stakes are so high, you don't know how to make them a second time. This was one of those mistakes.

I took him through the closet to the louvered doors. The bedroom had a futon and a night table from a thrift store. White blinds over the windows covered the view to the overgrown side driveway.

I pointed at the half-open door to the bathroom. It was done in pink marbelite and floral wallpaper. The house hadn't been redone since the 1960s, and the new owners were soon-to-be rock stars blowing their wad on converting half the building to a studio. No one had time for swanky bathrooms.

Hawk smiled at me and flipped his sunglasses to the top of his head. His eyes were red-rimmed and older than his years.

"It's over there." I pointed again and turned to walk back into the hall. I wanted to see what Strat was doing. It was a compulsion I didn't understand, but if he was going to fuck someone, I wanted to see it. See her. Or them. Just to make sure I'd completely lost him.

Hawk didn't go to the bathroom, and I was so lost in my own thoughts and intentions—again, you could see this coming a mile away—that when he grabbed my arm, I was annoyed, not scared.

"What?" I was still being polite, so I cut the sharpness out of my voice.

"You're really cute," he said, lightening his grip a tiny bit.

"Thanks."

"Sexy. Got a really smart mouth. I like that."

"You can let me go now."

He did. I was relieved about that for half a second because he closed the patio door.

I crossed my arms and leaned heavily on one foot. "Dude, I'm not watching you pee. Not my thing, all right?"

"What's your thing?" He stepped closer to me, tongue flicking his bottom lip the way it did when he played guitar. The girls loved that. They went nuts. But he wasn't my thing.

"My thing is getting a beer."

Oh, Jesus, that was what he was after? My thing. Indiana was my thing. Strat was my thing. Those two assholes made me feel so damn good and they barely even touched me.

"How do you like it?" His hand reached for me, and I curved away.

"I like it on Wednesdays. Today's Saturday. Sorry. My legs are closed for business."

I tried to get around him, but his hand shot out and gripped my jaw. He pressed his fingers together, and my mouth opened. I bent my knees trying to get away, but he held me up.

"Your mouth's open like a dick-shaped hole."

Did I mention he was a brilliant lyricist?

I grunted and pushed him away, and he slammed me between the wall and his body, his erection pressed against me. The first hard-on I'd ever felt. I squeaked.

He held two little blue capsules in front of my eyes. I tried to focus, but my entire face hurt from his grip.

"You're going to love this." He popped one capsule in his mouth and jammed the other one to the back of my throat. "Swallow."

I shook my head, trying to scream and failing. He pressed my jaw closed. I tried to breathe, letting the weight go from my legs, but he wrestled himself down with me. I slapped his face, and he took it with a snarl.

"You like it rough. I knew it. I could tell."

I couldn't move. We were crouched in a corner, his knees and the hand on my mouth leveraged against the wall. His face was slick with sweat, and his tongue kept licking a dry spot on his lips.

I *hmphed* against his hand. If I spit enough, maybe it would slide off of my face. Maybe someone in the party would hear me scream over the music. But the extra spit dissolved the gelatin capsule, and my mouth was flooded in bitter juice.

"Good girl," he said.

If I'm so good, why are you still holding me down?

I couldn't say that with his hand over my mouth. If I could move before the Quaaludes took effect, I could get to Strat or Indy and they'd protect me. But once they were in my blood, I'd be high and horny. I wouldn't be myself. I'd probably open my legs like it was Wednesday.

He could fuck any girl he wanted. That party was full of pussy for guys like him. Why me? I wanted to ask, but he still had his hand over my mouth. The other hand pulled my knees apart.

"You're such a pretty little thing. Think you're so tough. Everybody wants you. Did you know? We talk about it. How we want you and you don't give it up. Well, now we can talk about how I got you to give it up."

I breathed hard through my nose, my hands curled into his jacket. I didn't know how to get away as he kept saying things meant to flatter and arouse me.

"I see those nipples under your shirt. So tight. Baby, you're so sexy. You're gonna want it so bad in a few minutes. You're gonna beg for it. Don't fight it." He pushed his hand up the inside of my thigh, fingers reaching into my shorts, touching my skin. My actual pussy.

I kicked, and one of my denim wedges came off.

"See?" he said. "Not dipped in gold."

I squealed and squirmed anew, and he got the crotch of my shorts in his fist and pulled. I slid onto the carpet, and my shorts came down to mid-thigh. I opened my mouth to scream, but he shoved four fingers in it, blocking the sound.

There was a slap from somewhere, and I thought he'd hit me, but I was wrong. I could smell and hear the party, and suddenly Hawk was off me. I gulped for air. I pushed him away but only swung in the air. I was just completing an action I couldn't a second before.

"Hey, man!" Hawk shouted, but it was too late.

He bounced off the closet door, and Strat punched him in the face. The two girls from the kitchen were in the doorway. The one with a lipstick-smeared face ran away, and the other stood in shock and horror as Strat pulled his fist back again. The muscles of his back tensed and stretched, moving the musical staffs like undulating waves.

It landed with a crunch. The girl screamed and looked at me, which was when I realized my shorts and underwear were right above my knees.

"Tell him you wanted it!" the girl screeched from the doorway.

"What?"

"He's gonna kill him!" she shouted.

As if in answer, I heard a crack and the closet doors rattling. I tried to get up, and my hand landed on one of my denim wedges. I landed on my elbow.

I didn't feel anything. That was my normal state of being, but this particular numbness covered confusion and hurt. I got to my knees as Strat hit Hawk again.

The girl who had been in the doorway was pretty brave. She got between the two and tried to push Strat away. She definitely made it harder for him to get a clear shot, and the time she bought was enough to get Indy in the room.

It all happened so fast, with such complexity, that my shorts were still down. That's what stopped Indy in his tracks. Not the blood smeared across the Grammy-winner's face. Not his partner's pulled back fist. But me. My naked body.

Shit.

I pulled up the shorts.

Indy turned to Strat and put his hand on his shoulder and pushed, wedging himself between Strat and his punching bag.

"What's happening?" Indy said it so gently, it was a harmony of a hundred thousand heavenly tones.

"Fuck him." Strat spun to me, and Indy followed.

I was on my knees, butt-to-heels, arms crossed over my chest. "I'm fine."

"You are not fine." Strat's words were clipped.

With his eyes, Indy took me in, then his friend, then turned to Hawk, who was just getting his feet under him with the help of the girl with the smeared lipstick.

"Get out," Indy said, swinging his arm wide. "All of you. Out." Indy helped me up. He looked me in the eye. "What did he give you?"

"Lude."

He shook his head. "I wish Strat killed him."

Oh fuck. Was I going to cry?

For the love of fuck.

Stop it.

He put his hand on the back of my neck. The next thing he said was so gentle and strong, and his voice sounded like a layer of gravel floating on the deep blue sea.

"You're safe now."

The sea rose, moved forward, curved to bubbling white at the top, and dropped on me. I couldn't stop the stream of emotions any more than I could have used matchsticks to hold up a tidal wave.

Feelings. Joy. Lust, fear, gratitude surprise arousalhatedisgustangerlovelovelove.

Lubricated with Quaalude and a narrowly avoided rape, they crushed me into sentence fragments. I couldn't get anything out that made sense. I was crying a flood of shit I'd held on to for months. Maybe years. Maybe forever.

The room was empty except for Indy and me. Strat had taken Hawk out by the collar. Indy had shouted *out* and closed the door behind all the gawkers.

Indy took me by the chin and looked in my eyes. It was getting dark, and I was covered in tears, but he saw enough to let my face go. "They're dilating already."

I'm fine. I thought it but couldn't speak.

He picked me up from the shoulders and under the knees. My other wedge fell off as he carried me

where are you taking me

to the futon, where he tried to set me down

I don't think so

but I held onto his neck and pulled him down until his face filled my vision

see? I'm not crying anymore

and he put me down but stayed close. He looked reluctant, but his pupils were like bowling balls. He was with me on whatever plane I was on. The pupils didn't lie. He'd popped whatever I'd been fed, or some other inhibition-reducing drug.

is it now? Make it now

He smelled like a man. My brain wasn't making sentences but

musk and sweat and chlorine from the pool

the scent alone drove a spike of desire between my legs so hard it was almost painful. I arched my back from it, and my eyes fluttered and my lips parted and

"It's the lude, Cin."

everything felt good while the potential for more good feeling seemed like a limitless void I could fill right now, right there. I put my hand between my legs and rubbed myself over my shorts because

oh God so good so good

all the void was inside me, and I had to fill it up. He had to fill it up. He had to. He was beautiful, and I loved him. The little voice inside my head that said that was the drugs talking. I knew that voice was on to something, but I didn't care.

I took Indy's hand and put it between my legs. I was so hot he sucked air between his teeth when his fingers landed there.

"I want you," I whispered, suddenly aware enough to put together three words.

"No, you don't. It's the—"

"The lude. I know. I can say what I feel."

I spread my legs and

are you really doing this?

moved his hand under the crotch, and his fingers pushed the rest of the way through, until he felt how wet I was.

"Holy—"

"Oh my—"

"—shit."

"—God!"

He ran his fingers along my seam, and the second time over my clit, I exploded, mouth open, silent, muscles tightening, knees bent.

It was the most powerful, yet unsatisfying orgasm I'd ever had. I needed more. I was empty. Full of emotions. Full of joy and lust and a swirling ambition, and in the vortex of those was a centripetal void shaped like his body.

He thought for a second/million years and put his lips on mine, opening his mouth, giving me his tongue.

This is it.

I trusted him. The weight of his body, the thrust of his hips pushing the shape of his dick to me. I grinded against him as if it was my job. I was going to come all over again, clawing at his shirt, pulling it over his head. The arousal was so deep I couldn't see past it.

"How old are you, Margie?"

"Eighteen." I pulled off my tank top. "Give or take." I wasn't in the habit of wearing a bra, and I didn't even have the shirt all the way off before I felt his teeth on my nipples.

"I'm twenty," he said.

"Nice to meet you."

He pulled my shorts and underpants off in one move and kneeled between my open legs. His bare chest had a dusting of brown hair and a tattoo of a treble clef with a bird over his heart. I reached for his waistband, but my arms weren't long enough.

He grabbed my wrists and put them over my head, pressing them to the wall, and kissed me. "I've wanted you for a long time."

"I know."

"I shouldn't," he said. "You're not straight."

"Neither are you."

"True, true."

He rolled off me and lay on his back. He hooked his thumbs in his shorts, picked up his butt, and pushed them off.

His dick.

My heart dropped to below my waist. I wanted that beautiful thing. Maybe I did have a dick-shaped hole because it went on fire at the sight of it. I straddled him as soon as the shorts were off.

It was the lude. I couldn't even think. He pushed me down, the length of him on the length of my seam, rubbing where I was wet. I slid up and down, a tease of the act itself.

"Ludes make you come so many times," he said. "So do it. Come now."

The words. I didn't know what words could do. The

permission cast a shadow with the light of inhibition. I ran myself against him, clit to cock, and came again, fingers digging into his shoulders. I took a breath to wonder if I was doing it right. I looked to him for cues and knew I must be all right because he was biting his lower lip, pushing against me.

Sex was so good, and I was still a virgin.

"Yes," I said. "Let's go."

"You're so hot. So hot." He took his dick by the base and shifted it to me.

I positioned myself over him then

this is it, Margaret

pushed down. His face knotted with concern when

now or later but now is better

we hit resistance but

"Wait," he said.

I pushed down hard, and something ripped. Something hurt. I froze for a second with him buried inside me, surprised at the stretching pain at my opening and the snug fit inside.

"You didn't tell me." He breathed it, gritting his teeth not in anger but a need to keep his head on straight against the knowledge that his head wasn't his own.

I needed him. I couldn't pretend I was experienced or even competent. I'd seen what I'd seen and knew what I knew, but it wasn't enough. The Quaalude made me eager and optimistic, flooded with the feeling that nothing could go wrong.

"Show me what to do now," I said.

He took me by the back of the neck and pulled me over him until I was an inch from his 33rpm eyes and I could taste the whiskey on his breath.

"I don't want to hurt you."

"I'll already remember you forever. You gonna make it count or what?"

He stroked my cheek with his thumb. His words were hard, but his tone was a caress. "Are you sure you don't have a set of balls somewhere?"

"You should be the last one to ask that."

"You're really special, Margie. You don't need me. You

don't need anyone. That's what I was afraid of all this time, that I'd end up inside you and I'd never see you again."

How many minutes had passed since Hawk made me swallow? Fifteen minutes? Twenty? The room had gone from deeply angled sun to a wash of blue, yet time was nothing.

I didn't understand any of what I was feeling. The unmotivated elation caused by the drug I'd been force-fed was a bucking stallion behind a wood fence. With every kick, the lock bent. Soon the fence was going to crash down in a splintered heap and I was going to promise him an eternity together for another and another and another orgasm.

"Do I move like this?" I shifted my hips in a circle and drove down until I felt a pressured pain deep inside and my clit rubbed against him.

He groaned. That was good. He took my hips and shifted me up then down again.

"Like that," he said, hands running up my waist to my tits. He pinched them, and a new shot of pleasure ran down my spine.

I moved up then down until he was deep in me.

"Push against me here." He took a hand off my tit to press the front of me against him, so my nub rubbed against his body.

I gasped.

"When you come up, angle yourself so you get it the whole way. Go."

I did what he said, letting my clit feel the length of him. "Oh, God. That's. Fuck."

We moved slowly, up and down, pressing deep, the friction and pressure bringing me close to a third orgasm.

"If I make you come on your first time—"

"Gold star. Fuck. God. Gold star it's so good."

"You have to come soon. Please come soon I'm so-close-no-I'm-there." His eyes closed, and his jaw got tight.

I thought the drug had made me feel good already. I thought it had aroused me more than normal, but I wasn't even halfway there. The bucking stallion of emotion broke through the gate, and I was blindsided by a rush of joy. I cried out from the chest-bursting, brain-exploding emotional high. My world washed bright yellow, and as I dropped down on his dick, deep and hard, my orgasm flooded orange, deep red, explosive, centered on cunt and mind, mixing at the heart of something so vivid I couldn't see who I was past it.

I dropped on top of him, barely breathing. His chest heaved under me.

"Gold star," I gasped. "I'll remember you forever."

He laughed. "You haven't even started to remember me."

CHAPTER 20.

1983

Strat died about six months after the last time I saw him, and I found out about it six months after that. I was in the library, catching up on schoolwork with a newfound ambition.

The library magazine rack was in front of my Debate Team materials, and I stopped when I saw Strat's music-strewn bare chest on it. I bit my lower lip. I'd been home a month and hadn't called him or Indy. I didn't want to explain about the baby or whose it was (or wasn't). I didn't want to revisit any of it. I was a new woman.

But he was majestic, and the photo was dark in a way that made it mysterious. I was curious.

CHAPTER 21.

1982 – The morning after the night of the Quaalude

The morning after I'd had a Quaalude shoved down my throat, I woke up on the couch with a headache. Indy was already in the kitchen, slogging down a glass of water.

"Where'd you go last night?" he asked.

"Good morning to you too." The light tasted too yellow. The air hurt. The floor and sky were too loud.

"Here." He shook three aspirin out of the bottle into my palm. The circles were too perfect and too white, the big B etched into them too capitalized.

He filled a glass of water for me. I washed the pills down and drank the entire glass.

"Thank you," I said, handing the cup back.

He took it then took my wrist and pulled me toward him. Bone creaked on bone, but it didn't hurt. I let myself lean on him.

"I have to tell you something." He spoke into my ear and stroked my back. That didn't hurt either.

"Mmm."

"I want to take another crack at last night, but without the ludes."

"Mm-hmm."

"Or Strat."

I swallowed.

Jesus.

Last night.

I hadn't forgotten as much as I'd woken up feeling like I

had Dengue fever or something. But, yeah. Last night had happened.

I leaned back until I could see his eyes. "I think I just need to sleep today."

"Are you okay to stay?"

I shook my brain. Yes. I was supposedly on a camping trip. I hated camping, but I'd had to lie.

Right? I had to wrap my life in lies.

"Indy, I have to tell you something. After I tell it to you, you're never going to want to see me again."

He did something that took my breath away. He leaned over and swept my feet from under me, getting his arm under my knees. "Never tell me. Never say it."

His lips tightened a little, and without saying a word, I was sure he knew.

"Are you sure?"

"Yes."

I help up my hand. "Open pledge."

He laughed, and though it was loud, it didn't hurt my head. "My hands are occupied. Assume it's up."

"Swear you don't want to know. Swear you're already okay with whatever I was going to say."

"I do. Close pledge."

I slung my arm around his neck, rested my head on his shoulder, and let him carry me to his room.

I had a life in the weeks that followed, but not much outside Drew. I helped with the studio, hammering and painting, getting boxes and running cables. I could have done that forever, lost the world and gained my soul.

But there wasn't a soul to be had.

CHAPTER 22.

1994

"Evidentiary privileges," Drew said, sliding a box up high.

I gave him the next one. It was after dark, but we were almost done. I'd spent the entire process watching the veins on his forearms, the way his biceps strained his shirt, the movement of his lips when he spoke.

"I just did that one," I complained.

"You don't get to stop until you can bill two-fifty an hour. Evidentiary privileges."

I picked up another box and brought it to him. They weren't heavy. "Attorney-client. Doctor-patient. Spousal. Priest-penitent."

He pushed the box to the topmost position in the pile, and I gave him the last one.

"Done." I slapped my hands together.

"Contracts, quick—"

"You can't go from evidence to contracts like—"

"Construction. Give me rescission remedies."

I put my hands on my hips. He was making it hard, and I loved it. "Builder in breach. No remedy. Owner in breach. Builder gets market value of work done."

He stepped toward me. "Land sale," he said in a velvety, non-demanding tone.

"Payments less land value."

He touched my elbows, pulling them toward him, so they weren't impatient angles on my hips. "Sale of goods."

I let my arms go around his waist. I wanted him right there, on a stack of boxes, breathing mildew and old air. I'd been with a few guys since Ireland, but I'd never felt so comfortable. Had he only been back in my life a day? Had it been just that morning when he knocked into me in the waiting room? I felt as though we'd picked up where we left off.

"Are we still in rescission?" I purred.

"You're really cute when you're buying time."

"The contract is canceled and either party can sue for breach."

I tilted my head up, breathing in his Drew/Indiana-ness. I could practically taste him.

"Not quite." He spoke in breaths, his lips grazing my face. "Non-conforming goods need to be established before cancellation and injunctive relief."

Our lips were going to touch on "injunctive." I was on my toes, leaning up, my hands feeling the tightness at his waist.

But when thunder ripped through the air and rain suddenly pattered on the windows, I jumped too far back for him to reach.

"Crap," I said.

Without a word, we scrambled to the two boxes we'd put outside. He put them into the trunk of his Audi rental, and we scrambled inside.

"Where are you staying?" I asked. "I mean... just..."

"They have me in a condo in Century City."

The firm had apartments for visiting clients. They must use them for visiting attorneys as well.

"That's across town from the office," I stated the obvious. For clients, Century City made sense. For an employee, it was stupid.

"I get the real Los Angeles experience, traffic and all." He started the car. "Where are you headed?"

"I live in Culver, but my car is downtown, and I have a family thing tonight in Malibu."

"That's a mess," he said.

"I can get a cab Downtown."

At rush hour, then I had to head west. I'd get to dinner

with everyone after ten, and I wouldn't see my brother. He was having trouble at school, and though it wasn't my job to correct it, I was the only one he listened to.

Mostly, I didn't want to get a cab downtown. I wasn't done with Drew.

I spoke before I thought it out. "Are the partners taking you to dinner tonight?"

"That was last night."

"Come to dinner at my family's place then. You can ogle the size of it. We have a great cook, and I have seven siblings to play with. If you like kids, that is."

"I love kids."

Of course he did.

CHAPTER 23.

1982 – Five weeks after the night of the Quaalude

The pregnancy test was in my bag, a big square lump on a heavier lug of books. I didn't usually carry all my things. We usually bought a separate set of textbooks for home, so all I had to carry were my notebooks. But I had to hide that stupid test. The nannies and housekeepers had started looking suspicious of my comings and goings, and I never knew when one of them was going to innocently (or not so innocently) slip or snoop.

The band had gone to Nashville to meet with a producer. Two weeks. Perfect. I was supposed to get my period in that time.

But I didn't.

On the day the boys were set to return from Nashville, I got a beep from the Palihood house number. I went up there with my backpack and without a plan. I didn't know what to tell them. I couldn't even take the test until the next morning, so what did I expect? What did I want? Should I even tell them I was all of nine days late for my period? I mean, so what? I'd been late before. My schedule was all screwed up. What was the point of worrying them into thinking I was going to ask them for anything besides the number of an abortion clinic?

The side door was unlocked, and I walked in unannounced as always. I thought of putting my bag by the door, but the elephant in the room had been zipped into it, so I kept it slung over my shoulder.

I was about to walk into the kitchen because the beer and

cigarettes were there, but I felt a vibration in the floor. Standing still, I listened. Birds. The freeway. The ticking of the clock. Men talking behind walls. And music.

I went to the side of the house I'd only seen down to the studs.

The studio was sheetrocked and painted. Floors down. Gold record and band photos hanging in the hall. The window to the isolation booth sealed and egg-carton-shaped soundproofing on the walls.

Strat stood in front of the mic, copper-gold hair tied at the base of his neck, unleashing a note I couldn't hear. The door to the adjacent engineering room was ajar. I peered inside. Indy sat at the control panel while a goateed guy I'd seen around untangled some wires.

"Dude," Indy said into the mic, looking at Strat through the window.

"Dude," Strat said into his own mic. "Really?"

"Warm as the girl in the middle," Indy replied joyfully.

My heart twisted once, sharply. I reprimanded myself. It was a metaphor, for Chrissakes. I told myself I didn't care. I had no feelings on the matter one way or the other. I liked Indy and he was fun, but only until he wasn't.

I didn't need to be special to him.

How much longer are you going to tell yourself that?

I opened the door before I could answer myself.

Indy turned. Then the engineer. The man whose baby I could have been carrying jutted his chin toward me in greeting then turned back to the egg-carton-lined room.

"Give me the next verse, Stratty." He jotted something in a notebook, not even looking at me when he said, "Close the door, Cin."

I closed it quietly and gently placed my bag on the couch behind the board as if a sleeping monster were inside it.

Strat wore a white T-shirt and black jeans with a chain that made a U from his front belt loop to his back pocket. It swayed with him as he sang. His voice was magic. It had been too long since I'd heard him.

"I need to talk to you guys," I said.

"I think we need to kill the preamp," Goatee said.

Indy moved a lever so slightly it could have been nothing at all. A low-level version of Strat's voice filled the room as he hummed to himself near the mic.

"No," Indy said, not even looking at me. "Make it work. We're not cheaping out on vocals."

"Sure, but…" a pentameter of technical terms I didn't understand followed.

Indy parried with another jumble of engineering nonsense, and Goatee thrust with his own as he counted a bunch of bills he'd pulled from his front pocket. My request for an audience had been denied apparently.

In the booth, Strat jotted notes, tapped his foot, and hummed verses.

I'd never felt like an outsider with them before, but I'd never seen them working either. It was a bad time. I'd come back after I did the test. Or not. But either way, I was doing what I had to with or without their permission.

I picked up my bag. When the handles got taut from the weight, I had to exert a little more energy to pull the whole thing up, and I wished I could lean on someone. I wished I hadn't always been so far removed, so cold, so non-demonstrative. I wished I was used to emotions because I was having them and I couldn't define them. They were moving through me so quickly I couldn't define them, much less cope with them.

I slung the bag over my shoulder and saw myself in the glass's reflection. I was translucent. Overlaid onto Strat's indifference.

I hated this. Needy. Childish. Whining. Grasping. Desperate. I saw myself from the outside. Out of control. Floundering. Hungry for validation. A few synonyms for "it's going to be all right" wouldn't cure me of the problem. Not even a little. So why did I want them so badly?

When I opened the door, Indy spun in his chair. "Didn't you want something?"

"It can wait."

I left, saving myself from myself. I could handle emptiness. I could handle solitude and isolation. This rush of neediness was going to kill me. If either one of them had started patting my head and saying he was going to help me/be there for me/whatever you want, baby, I would have told him to fuck off.

So when I heard Indy's voice behind me, I was tempted to just keep walking down the hall. But the needy part won. I turned to at least tell him, "No worries. I'm good." His posture, half in and half out of the engineering room, told me that would have been a welcome dismissal.

But I couldn't. That hot bubbling mess inside me wouldn't be silenced.

"You all right?" he asked.

I think I'm pregnant.

I'm sick in the morning.

"I'm fine. Welcome back."

"Thanks." He leaned back into the engineering room, and I took the opportunity to walk a few more steps down the hall, rescued and abandoned at the same time. "You coming back tonight?"

"Why?" I didn't turn around, keeping him at my back.

"Why?"

I didn't know how to answer. Didn't know how to move or think. I only knew how to blurt out my problems.

Something inside me feels like turned soil.

And I'm late.

And I knew how to shut myself up. I barely knew how to breathe without feeling the tension between breath and words.

"Yeah," I said. "Why?"

"Because we're back, and people are coming over. What's the problem, Cin?"

He wanted an honest fucking answer. He knew my fucking name, but he wouldn't even fucking use it.

Cin.

Cin, my ass. My fucking left tit. Taking my stupid stunt of a fake name and throwing it at me like a bucket of ice.

"You're working. We'll talk later."

If I'd been able to just walk away, things might have been different, but we were young. I had to offer him one chance to give me what I needed. But no, that wasn't to be. Indiana Andrew McCaffrey had to stake out his territory.

"Maybe." He waved at me dismissively, and with that, the potential to have my needs met went down the shitter.

"What do you mean maybe?"

"People come over, and it gets hard to talk. So it's cool."

I threw myself down the hall toward him, the weight of my bag pushing me forward, finger extended. "It's cool?"

He shrugged and looked back into the engineering room as if he was dying to get back in there. I'd never felt so alone in my entire life.

"Yeah."

"Don't you dare tell me you won't make the time to talk to me. I've never asked you for a goddamn thing, you—"

"That's fucking right." His tone was a cinderblock wall, and I shriveled inside even as I kept my own wall high and hard. "Look, if you're gonna turn crazy, you won't be the fucking first."

"What?"

"I'd be surprised. You didn't seem like the type. But before we 'talk,' I'm going to pull out what we said the night we met. Feelings aren't real, so we don't bother. Right? You're not getting crazy. Right?"

Crazy. The world and everyone in it was crazy. Because I had feelings. I didn't know what they were or who they were even for. Maybe I had feelings for a way of life that was about to end.

"Look," he said, rubbing his lower lip with his thumb. A little swipe of discomfort. "We're really busy right now. There's no time for this."

Whatever my feelings were, Indy wasn't going to help me sort them out, and fuck him. I didn't need him or his help. He didn't even know what to do with his own damned feelings.

"Better get back to work," I sneered.

I took my crazy and went down the hall without looking back.

Fuck him seven ways to Sunday.

Fuck both of them.

CHAPTER 24.

1994

The Audi cut through the rain like a machete, and Drew drove as if he lived in a place where it rained more than two months out of the year. I felt safe. Again.

"I saw you in *Rolling Stone*," I said as if I was just trying to make conversation. I flipped through a black wallet of CDs. Doubtless a small fraction of what he had at home.

"That was such a joke."

"Too redemptive?"

"I did half the drugs they said I did."

"That's still a lot."

He smiled. "Yeah. There was plenty. It was the eighties. What can I tell you? I was a wreck. *Sound Brothers* was making a ton of money, and I was wrecked over Strat."

I slid a disc from the sleeve. *Kentucky Killer.* The album that turned me into a groupie and got them the deal that financed the studio. The one with the masters in the trunk of the car.

"I'm sorry about that," I said.

He shrugged and looked in the rearview before changing lanes as if he needed something to do with his hands and mind. "Yeah, thanks. I just... I didn't know. After you were gone, we started fighting. Bad shit. Fistfights. I don't know what was wrong with him. Or me. Maybe it was me. I think about it a lot. Was it all really my fault? I mean, he blamed me for letting you go. He said he wouldn't have. So I shut down. I didn't even want to look at him. I got very involved with the studio. He had the business head, and I kept just wanting to do shit my way."

"You made the studio a real success."

"I never felt like that without him. Feels like I'm treading water most days. He said the studio should be passive. It should run itself while we made music, and I just kept getting more and more involved in the day-to-day. I could barely show up to our own sessions, and Gary had a kid, so he was checked out. Strat just lost it. Went back to Nashville."

"It wasn't your fault."

"It wasn't. He had a bad heart. Congenital aortic valve something. If he knew, he might have decided to take too much heroin instead of amphetamines."

"Was that supposed to be funny?"

"Yeah."

"It was."

I'd mourned Strat's death. He'd died from only a slight overdose of uppers. His heart couldn't take it. I'd thought about that too deeply, reading too much into a heart that couldn't stand the exertion. I sought out details about his demise to avoid the sadness. I told myself he was a jerk, that he didn't matter, that he was in my distant past. But it did matter. A haze followed me, because he was indeed my past. I'd owned that life, that past, those stories that built me, and it all went and died while I wasn't looking.

"He cared about you," Drew said, glancing at me before he put his eyes back on the freeway. "We went to meet you on Santa Monica and Vine. And that neighborhood..." He shook his head. "Of all the corners to pick. We didn't know if you'd been dragged into an alley and murdered."

I shot out a laugh at how close to the truth he was. "I'm sorry I flaked."

"You didn't flake. We went to your house—"

I sat ramrod straight, eyes wide, adrenaline flooding my veins. "You did not."

"Did. We got a lawyer to find out where you lived, and we got ten different kinds of runaround. Then a guy with a gun and a badge opened the door. He flashed an order of protection and made threats. We stopped coming around."

"They never told me."

Of course they hadn't told me. I was indisposed and powerless.

"I'm sorry," I said, looking at my open hands as if I was trying to set the past free. "I just couldn't take it anymore. I…"

Deep breath.

This is important.

"I just needed to start over."

"I was an asshole to you," he said.

"You were fine. It was me. I was in over my head."

"We figured you weren't dead, so we just… well, we didn't forget. I let it go, but I didn't forget. Figured it was the way I'd talked to you the last time I saw you. Strat was pissed off. He was the one you called, and he insisted you sounded upset. I told him Cin didn't get upset. Cin is together. She never lets her feelings get the better of her. But he swore up and down. He paid a detective to watch the house until the day he died."

"Eight months after I flaked."

"You didn't flake."

"How do you know?"

"I know you. If you needed to get away from us, I get it. That's not flaking."

I made a breath of a laugh. He knew me. Sure. I always did what I said. If I said "meet me at Santa Monica and Vine," then I was going to get off the bus at Santa Monica and Vine with my smallest Louis Vuitton suitcase.

The rain pounded the windows, marbleizing them to opacity. The windshield wipers did nothing to break the stream. I gripped the edge of the leather seat because the red lights ahead of us got too big too fast.

Drew snapped the right blinker on to get off the freeway. It was miles too soon, but it was the only safe option.

He would have been a good father.

I covered my face with my hands. Did I steal that from him?

Note to self: "Not feeling" stuff doesn't mean you're not

feeling it. Being unemotional and cold doesn't mean you don't have a pot full of emotions waiting to boil over. It means the heat hasn't been turned up enough, and the pot just hasn't been there long enough. It means the pot hasn't reached capacity.

But it will.

And your heart will beat so fast and hard you'll want to die. Your eyes will flush with tears, and your throat will close like a valve's been turned. Regret will fill you on a cellular level until the very tips of your fingers tingle with self-loathing.

"I'm sorry," I said.

He parked the car and shut it off. "You didn't make the rain. Just give it ten minutes."

"No. I'm sorry I didn't flake. I'm sorry I didn't tell you what happened. I'm sorry I left you there. I'm just sorry for everything."

"Margie? What's happening?"

He put his arms around me, but I pushed him away violently. Once I told him, he would be sorry he'd ever touched me.

"I was pregnant."

I could see the entire diameter of his blue eyes as he looked at me in surprise, jaw slack, expression otherwise empty. Was it surprise? Was I wrong in thinking he already knew? Or was that wishful thinking?

I swallowed putty, looked into the pouring rain, and ground my teeth until I could breathe enough to speak. "I was going to meet Strat and get an abortion because I didn't want you to talk me out of it, and I was so damn mad at you. After I called, I tried to get to you. I climbed out of my bedroom window, but my parents caught me in the driveway and sent me away."

He shook his head, eyes narrowed as if I'd just dropped a bomb in his brain and he had to make sense of the pieces.

"Do not pass Go," I continued. "Right to LAX. A fucking convent in Ireland. I'm sorry. I'm so sorry. I should have called when I got back. But I was fucked in the head, and I couldn't deal."

He got a white handkerchief out of his pocket, and I snapped it away to wipe my eyes. It didn't even begin to do the job.

"Where's the baby?" he asked, pointing at the elephant in the room.

"Adopted."

"Where?"

"Jesus, Indiana! How the fuck should I know?"

He looked out his side window, probably so he wouldn't have to look at me.

"My parents came to Ireland during my last trimester to set up the adoption, so the baby's probably there."

Funny how I still thought of it as a baby. He or she had to be Jonathan's age already.

Drew looked back at me, all the surprise and distance gone.

"My mom was really pregnant too, which was just great because she hated me for getting knocked up at the same time. She had her baby in the hospital, then I had mine in the convent, and Dad just took it. I didn't even hear it cry. A week later, they took me home. Mom had post-partum. Dad acted like the whole thing had been a fun trip and the bad shit never happened. Which, you know, I'll admit that worked for me."

The shadows of the rain fell on the curves of his beautiful face in an overlay of wrinkles and age. Yet he looked twenty again, an overwhelmed artist on the verge of a life of riches and fame. A kid with nothing but mistakes to make. He'd seen a lot. He'd lost his best friend. Faced the death of his father and the surrender of his mother. He'd been strong for his family even when all the perks and goodies of a life in the spotlight tempted him away.

And I hadn't given him a thought.

I'd been so wrapped up in my own problems for eleven years that I hadn't thought about him or what he needed. Wasn't he as much a part of this as I was? Didn't he have the right to know? To claim what was his?

Well, there was that.

"It never occurred to me to find you. I was thinking about

what was easy for me. And even when I saw you in the office... I was still thinking about myself. I'm sorry."

I didn't want him to speak, but that was the problem, wasn't it? I'd never wanted him to speak. I'd wanted him to go away. In the front seat of his rented Audi, with the rain pounding the glass, that changed. I wanted to know what he thought. I'd suffer the slings and arrows he threw at me if he'd just say what was on his mind.

He opened his mouth to speak, and I'd admit I flinched a little.

I wanted him to like me, to want me, to love Cin again and learn to love Margie. I should have felt like a little whiney bitch for that, but I didn't. I didn't have the energy to berate myself for wanting to be wanted.

"And..." he started, and I braced myself, "who were you thinking about when you invited me to a family dinner?"

It was crazy to laugh, but I did. I wasn't used to having this fucked up soup in my guts. I was off balance from the pendulum of emotion. Walking on a lubed-up balance beam. Of course I fell, but at least I fell on the side of laughter. If I cried another tear, I was going to have to wring out his hankie.

"Me!" I said. "I wanted to spend time with you again, and I was totally thinking of myself. But you look different. And we can call you Drew and never even talk about what happened. They won't know."

"But I'll know."

I stopped in the middle of a lateral mood swing. Just froze.

He wasn't talking about the baby and whatever right he had or didn't think he had to it. No. His face wasn't hurt or victimized. It was rigid with rage.

"Don't pretend it's about me," I said.

"Why not?"

"Just don't." I was almost screaming. I sounded crazy. Drunk on *feelings*.

"It's about you."

"No, it's—"

"Did anyone stand up for you? All this time? Has anyone—

"

I couldn't hear another word. I yanked the door handle. It slipped with a deep clack. I grunted and pulled it again, even as Drew reached over to close the door.

Neither the downpour nor the unknown neighborhood slowed me down. I didn't care about my work shoes or the cold rain that soaked my white shirt. I was sodden before I got three steps away from the car.

I didn't expect him to pull away and leave me there. I figured I'd grab a cab or find a payphone while he stayed in the car and followed me. Because who would run out into this shitstorm? What normal person would leave the car running, the headlights on, and jump into a fucking monsoon to grab my arm?

"Let me—"

"Shut up!" he shouted, already soaked, hair flat on his scalp, eyelashes webbed with water. His shirt stuck to him, translucent enough to reveal the treble clef over his heart. "For once, shut that mouth and listen. I never forgot you. Never. Not a day went by in that studio without me thinking about you. How you think. How you talk. How you felt when I was inside you."

"You shut up! You forgot me, and you should have."

"I didn't."

"I was nothing." I jabbed my finger at him. "I was a short-term habit."

He continued as if I hadn't even spoken, water dripping from the angles of his face, along his cheekbones and jaw, meeting at his chin and falling in a constant silver line. "When Strat died, I couldn't save him. I wanted you there. I needed you. As soon as you called him that night, I should have had the balls to go right to your house and get you. Now that I know what happened, I know it was the biggest mistake of my life. I'll always regret it."

"Then you're a fool."

"I am."

In the urban dark of the street, with only the headlights of the Audi illuminating the diagonal sketch marks of rain, I didn't see him move, but I tasted rain warmed by the heat of his mouth. He was too fast and was kissing me before I knew what was happening.

He kissed my breath away.

He kissed my defenses to dust.

His lips dared me to feel nothing.

He turned me from solid to liquid.

One hand cupped my chin, and the other pulled me close from the back of my neck, and fuck him fuck him fuck him because I put my hands on his chest again, to his shoulders, his neck, the back of his head. My fingers dug into his wet hair. I felt close to him again, as I had all the years before, when I held his heart in my hands and someone else threw it away.

"I'm not abandoning you again," he said between kisses, running his face over my cheek like the water that spilled over it.

"Don't be stupid."

"Please. Let me earn this."

I pushed him away. His right eye was crystalline in the headlamps, bathed in light and rain.

"You've lost it, Indiana."

"I have. Slowly. Since I saw you this morning."

My teeth chattered as I looked him up and down. I didn't know what to make of him. I didn't know what to feel.

"I used you," I said, speaking the truth to myself as well as him. "I was looking for bad things to do, and you were there. I used you to fuck myself up."

"I know." His treble clef heaved under the wet fabric, a scar from a dream he'd once had. The footprint of a thing he'd loved and lost.

"I can see right through your shirt," I said. "It's indecent."

He pulled me to him, and we ran back to the car. He opened the door for me, and I leaned over inside and popped open the driver's door. It had barely closed behind him when he stretched across the seat and kissed me again. I put my hand on his wet chest, and he put his up my skirt. I let him, wrangling my body around his, opening my legs for his touch.

"That's not the rain," he said, sliding a finger inside me.

"God, no," I groaned. "It's you."

He drew his knuckles over my clit. "Look at me. Open your eyes and look at me."

His beard was soaked to dark brown, and droplets of water clung to his lashes. His hair stuck to his forehead.

"You're beautiful," I whispered. Then as he rubbed me again, I groaned, driving my hips forward. "Take me."

I reached between his legs and felt him. He sucked a breath through his teeth.

"We're not done." He yanked his belt open. "I'm going to fuck you right here, right now. But it's not the last time. Do you hear me?"

"Yes."

I would have promised him beachfront property in Nevada, especially after he took his dick out.

I wiggled out of my underwear while he reached into his wallet for a condom. Good man. No need to make the same mistake twice. I swung my leg over him, positioning him under me.

He pressed the head of his cock at my entrance with one hand, and with the other, he took my jaw. "This is not the last time. Say you understand."

"I do. I get it. I swear."

Was I lying? Maybe. But he was pressed against me, and every nerve ending between my legs vibrated for it.

"Say it."

"This is not the last time."

He pushed me down, entering me slowly.

"Look at me," he whispered again.

"You feel so good. It's hard to keep my eyes open."

"Feel it, Margie. Feel it."

He pushed me onto him, driving down to the root, every inch a reminder of what we'd had and what we were—a reimagined beginning with a past that ended us.

CHAPTER 25.

1983 After Ireland

Eighteen, give or take. Mostly take. I could get away with a lot because I looked and sounded like an adult, and in a lot of ways, I was. I didn't take shit, and I knew my own worth. That went a long way, but I was still as greedy as a child. I craved experiences. New things. Broken. Unraveled. Unwound. I could test the world. See what I could make anew.

I would have been a sociopath if I hadn't learned to give a shit when I got back from the cold stone convent in the old country. I'd eaten the shit sandwich I'd been fed, shed my rock groupie skin, and I acted like the oldest of eight.

The first time my mother put Jonathan into my arms, she looked nervous. She hadn't wanted me to touch him for the first week. Anyone else could, but not Margie. Maybe because he was the precious only boy of her eight children, but she handed him over as if I'd drop him or something. Or my irresponsible behavior would rub off on him. I didn't take it personally.

Post-partum wasn't properly diagnosed back then, so she was treated like a hysterical female, and I wasn't treated at all. I felt as if my guts had been ripped out and replaced with sawdust. I didn't eat. I didn't talk much. We were both in deep pain and acting as if nothing had ever gone awry.

Eventually I took Jonathan from the nurse while Mom napped. He was everything. He had a little tuft of red hair and crystal-blue eyes that would eventually turn green. I'd held just about all of my siblings, but there was something about

Jonathan. And the smell. Baby smell wasn't new, but his was different. It was the scent of heaven and earth. He held my finger with his tiny hand, and it didn't feel as though he did it out of newborn reflex. His grip felt like a plea. A connection. A deal rubbed with the salt of the earth.

I was going to make it my business to be there for him. To make myself useful if not to my own child, then to the brother born at the same time. I pledged it to him.

I straightened out so quickly, my family got whiplash. I never spoke to Lynn or Yoni again. I didn't make friends, but I made a few appropriate acquaintances.

It wasn't even hard.

"Did you breastfeed any of us?" I asked as Mom popped the bottle from Jonathan's mouth.

He was three months old, and I was still acclimating to my new life. Or my old life, depending on how you looked at it. It was the life a normal person my age should be living, not the life of someone who'd been whisked away to a foreign country to be tutored by stiff Irish nuns so she could secretly give birth to a baby she would never hold.

"Heavens, no. Why would I do that?" Mom handed the baby to the nanny to burp.

Her name was Phyllis, and she held her arms out but looked at me. She and I had set a pattern. Mom left before the baby kicked up his milk, and as soon as she was gone, Phyllis handed him to me. I slung him over my shoulder and patted his back, pressing my cheek to him so I could get a whiff of his baby smell. Best in the world.

I knew I was making Jonathan a replacement for the baby they gave away, but I couldn't help it. He smelled so good.

"I'll protect you, little brother," I whispered then put his little hand up against my own as if swearing on a stack of Bibles. "I pledge it."

I studied and behaved. I was a model of good and right behavior. I won my parents' trust back by staying in, helping my sisters with their homework, and finding a deep well of ambition.

You might think I was somehow browbeaten into good behavior. That I resented it. That I lost a wild part of myself to meet the expectations of others.

But it didn't feel like that. I felt wonderful. I helped Carrie and Sheila with their homework while Dad was off doing business and Mom was in her room. I wiped chocolate off Fiona's hands when she found the baker's cocoa in the back of the cabinet and ate the whole box.

I did everything but feed Jonathan. Mom insisted on feeding Jonathan until he started walking, then she abdicated, like with everything else. She was a figurehead, and oddly, I was okay with that. I loved her arm's-length parenting because she gave me room to fill my days with something meaningful to me.

Daddy was not an affectionate person, but after he spanked me for getting knocked up, he was never closer than half a room away. Even when I struggled in the back of the limo on the way to my flight to Ireland, he left the manhandling to an Italian bodyguard. He watched from the seats across with his jacket in his lap.

"One day," he'd said as Franco held me down, "one day you'll see this is for your own good."

I stuck my middle finger out at him.

"Who's the father?" he asked. "Who did this to you?"

I got my hand from under Franco's arm and stuck up my other middle finger.

"I'm going to find out."

All he'd have to do was dig around the groupie scene and he'd know, but he was so far removed from it, and I'd kept it so far away from my regular life, that I had hope he'd leave Strat and Indiana alone.

He sat next to me during the whole flight over. Just him, and he scared me. He checked me into the convent and left. They sent letters Sister Maureen made me answer. I said nice things, but I was shut down until he and Mom showed up three months before the baby was due.

"You look good," Mom had said. She was farther along

than I was.

I felt gross being next to her like that. "So do you. How do you feel?"

"Better than ever." She smiled and rested her hand on her belly. She loved being pregnant. I didn't know how she felt about raising children, but she loved carrying them. "We found a family for your baby. They live here. It's a good home."

"Thank you."

I hadn't fought that part of it. I didn't want to be a mother at that point, and I had no choice anyway. I was sure they'd done all the diligence in the world.

"Your friends miss you. They come by to let us know."

"Who came?"

She rattled off a few girls I knew from the Suffragette Society and Jenn from the Chess Strategy Club, then she looked at Dad.

He sat in the corner with an ankle crossed over his knee, staring at me. The movement of his head was barely perceptible, but he gave her a definite no to whatever she was asking. Mom was a lion when it came to everything except Dad. So she acted as though no one else had come, smiling as if our family dynamic was as normal as peas and carrots.

I went into labor three days early.

Dad was there when I gave birth, not Mom. I hadn't expected him to be in the room. I tried to ignore him, and once the pain got really bad, I could pretend he wasn't there. The midwife handed him the baby still slimy with goop.

"Is it a boy or a girl?" I'd asked, trying to catch my breath.

He didn't answer. No one answered. Sister Maura just shushed me, and Dad took it away. By the time I delivered the placenta, I knew they'd never tell me a thing.

I'd flown home alone. My sisters had greeted me like a long-lost child. Even my mother had been overcome with happiness when I walked in the door.

Dad seemed cautious. He treated me as if I were a museum artifact behind a velvet rope.

When I got into Wellesley, he congratulated me with a

handshake and a genuine smile, but he never touched me again.

I had to hang up a lot of my family duties when I went to Stanford Law, but I was always there. I called teachers when Fiona didn't understand her homework, chewed out Father Alfonso when he fire-and-brimstoned Deirdre, and tried to keep Jonathan inside the lines as he proved, time after time, that he could push every boundary with a cocky smile.

By the time I was studying for my bar, I felt as if the eighties were behind me. My parents had done their best, and I had a good life ahead. Sometimes I even felt gratitude.

CHAPTER 26.

1982 – The night of the Quaalude

I became enamored with the taste and feel of his nipples. The odd red hairs on his chest next to the brown ones. Quaaludes made you horny and happy, and we laughed a lot. I was getting ready to let him fuck me again. It hurt in a different way when he touched me. I was sore. But the internal pain had left.

I laid back and bent my knees, swinging them, smoking a cigarette. The cheap quilt under me felt good. Soft. Warm. Made for my skin.

And him. He was good. Very good. Kissing between my tits and down my belly. He was going to do to me the thing the girls had done with Strat. He was going to taste me. I tucked the cigarette between my teeth and put my fingers in his hair, spreading my legs for him.

When the door opened, I looked to see who came in but didn't move otherwise. I didn't jump or act ashamed, and neither did Indy.

"Dude," Strat said.

"Dude." Indy propped himself up on his elbows. "You get rid of Hawk?"

"Yeah. Party's over." Strat leaned down, plucked the cigarette from my lips, and put it between his own. He had no shirt, and the musical notations across his body curved around his nipples in a way I wanted to taste. "Said he gave you a blue lude. Looks about right."

"Yeah. Blue."

He blew out smoke.

I looked down at Indy, and he looked back up at me with a wicked smile.

"Naughty," I purred, reading his mind. I turned back to Strat and stretched, elongating my body, luxuriating in my nudity. I knew it was the drugs, and I didn't care. "You gonna give that back?"

He put the cigarette back in my mouth, peering down at me, through me, making some kind of calculation. I inhaled the delicious nicotine without touching the cigarette. Just sucking. Then I jutted my jaw at Strat. He took the butt from me and stamped it out in the ashtray on the floor.

"You're both luded," Strat said.

"Yup," Indy said then turned back to my belly.

I patted the mattress, staring at Strat. His long copper-red hair fell on each side of his face, and his jaw was rough with a day and a half of growth.

"Don't be a stranger," I said.

Strat glanced at Indy, who looked back at him intently and said, "You heard the woman."

The singer hesitated, looking from Indy to me. I'd never seen him hesitate before.

"I know you want to," Indy said. "One less thing to fight over."

In the seconds that passed, those two men who had grown up together and sacrificed for one another had a conversation without words. There had been a pledge, I knew that. But what was happening now?

I waited for what felt like hours but was probably breaths, and put one hand in Indy's hair while holding out the other to Strat. "Come on. It'll be fun."

I didn't think about the role reversal until years later, when I read about his death in *Rolling Stone*. Even then I smiled. I could practically taste him.

"Do what you want," Indy said. "But I'm eating this pussy right now."

And he did.

He opened my folds, exposing my clit. Even that felt good,

but when he laid his tongue on it, my neck arched.

"Oh, *God*!"

As if called by my prayer, Strat leaned next to the bed and kissed me. Not just kissed. He put his tongue in my mouth and claimed me. Indy brought me to orgasm with his mouth while I cried out into Strat's, a conduit from man to man. I lay there gasping, wanting more.

"Yes," Indy said, kneeling.

Strat was over me, pants down, cock out. So fucking hard and straight, I had to reach for it.

"You sure, Cinny?"

"Yes." I stroked him. I didn't know what I was doing, but it couldn't have been that bad.

"I want your ass. I'll try to make it good for you."

"I know."

Indy pulled me up to my knees, and I kissed him.

"Say you're sure to me," he whispered. "It's a lot for your first time."

"I want it now."

Behind me, Strat kneeled on the mattress and stroked my body. I felt his erection on my lower back.

"What about you?" I asked Indy.

"Yeah. But, Cin. Margie. I'm crazy about you. This doesn't change that. I want to know you."

I didn't tell him I wasn't knowable because the ludes made me feel elated and open, with years ahead of me that were going to start with these two men, on this mattress—now.

"Okay."

He smiled then got me under the arms and threw me on my back. "This is gonna be fun."

I laughed, and the next minutes were spent in some kind of heaven. The two of them covered me with their mouths and hands. Strat put his fingers in my mouth and I sucked them, groaning for him while Indy sucked my nipples to exquisite pain.

"Wet, Cin. Make them wet."

I did, licking between his second and third finger.

Strat pulled them out. "Good. You ready?"

"Yes."

I didn't actually know what I was supposed to be ready for until he bent my knees so deeply, Indy had to get off my tits and my hips lifted off the mattress. I was completely exposed, and they looked at me. Both of them. Indy played with my cunt, and Strat rubbed my ass with his wet finger. They watched my face.

The finger pressed forward, and my asshole yielded. I felt it everywhere. My entire body reacted with a shudder, tightening around him at the same time as my clit engorged. Indy slid two fingers into my pussy and leaned down to kiss me. I took the kiss, ate it, moaned into it, even when Strat got two fingers in me, burying them inside.

"Going for three," Strat said a million miles away. "Relax."

I'd never been so relaxed in my life, but that third finger broke through the high with a shot of pain. I tightened.

Indy took his mouth off me and turned to Strat. "Lube, asshole."

Strat flicked his hand at the night table. The same one the girl with the luscious hips had opened. Indy opened the drawer and found the same bottle of baby oil. He handed it over.

Strat popped it open. "Open up."

I lifted my knees, and Indy leaned over me and spread me wide. Cold, dripping oil fell on me, and the two of them spread it around, inside, outside. Making sure I was slick and ready, talking like two lawyers making sure every t was crossed and i was dotted.

I felt like the center of the known universe, swirling a galaxy of pleasure between my legs.

"Guys," I groaned. "That's so nice. Please."

"She's ready," Strat said to his childhood friend. He scooted back until he was sitting against the wall, cock out like a flagpole.

Indy helped me up. "Okay, face me on your knees."

He maneuvered me until Strat was behind me and could get his hands on my waist.

"Open," Strat said. "Pull it open."

My ass cheeks were slick with oil, but I dug in and opened them as Strat put pressure on my hips to lower me.

"Slow," Indy said.

"Slow, baby," Strat said.

Indy kneeled in front of me, eyes still dilated black, biting his lower lip as I went down until I felt Strat's dick against my ass. It seemed no different than the last barrier I'd broken that night, so I pushed down.

"Slow." Indy demanded when he saw my face. "We have all night."

It was different.

"Relax." Strat reached around and gently rubbed my clit.

Between the baby oil and my body's arousal, I was so wet that I didn't feel the least bit sore, and the pleasure relaxed me. My ass opened a little, and I bore down until the head was in. I stopped. Gasped.

"Can you take it?" Indy asked.

"Yes."

I got myself to a crouching position and lowered myself completely. Strat's cock went in all the way, and I continued down, down, stretching, taking every inch inside me. A sharp breath shot out of me with a crack of pain, but I didn't stop until he was rooted in my ass. Then I smiled, because I was stretched and full.

"So hot," Indy muttered, stroking his own cock.

I raised myself, feeling the sensation against the walls of muscle, then I went down again.

"That's it, baby," Strat said from behind me. "Take it. Take it hard."

"Indy?"

He took a deep breath and leaned forward. We shifted, realigned, and got my pussy right to take him. One hand on the wall behind us, one on my shoulder, he got his dick in.

It was a feeling I would never forget and one I never could repeat. All I had to do was stay still as they fucked me like two musicians with the same beat. One in, one out. Then both in at the same time.

Complete fullness. Stretched to my limit. Desired. Loved. Fucked endlessly everywhere. Both goddess and vessel.

"Touch yourself," Strat said. Neither of them had a free hand in the balancing act.

I jammed my fingers between Indy and me. I let out a long groan when I was close, but it was taking longer than I thought. It was too much. The pleasure wouldn't center where it needed to.

Indy put his nose astride mine and grunted into my cheek, exploding inside me.

I didn't think it was physically possible to feel any more pleasure or another slice of sensation, but I did, gathering vibrations between my fingers.

"Come, baby," Strat growled. "I want to feel it."

Indy pulled out and leaned back. His dick was slick with me and still stiff. "I got it."

He leaned down and flicked my clit with his tongue, then he sucked it hard as Strat pinched my nipples.

That was it.

As I screamed in pleasure, Strat pulled me down until he was deep inside me, and I came, ass pulsing around his cock.

"Ah, that's it," he groaned. "Fuck yes."

My orgasm was barely over when he pulled me up then slammed me down. Three, four, five times, then he came into me.

I leaned forward into Indy's arms, and we fell together, resting for fifteen minutes before we fell asleep in a heat of slick, euphoric flesh.

CHAPTER 27.

1994

"I thought you were going to be the easy one," I said. The rain had lightened to dime-sized splats and rushing veins on the windshield. The inside of the car smelled of salt water and sticky tar.

"What's that supposed to mean?" Drew asked, brushing his fingers through his hair as he drove. It had loosened from its stiff lawyer-do and fell in his face the way it used to.

I'd settled into a mellow trust with him. The same zone as I'd fallen into eleven years earlier. "Strat was like an animal in a jungle. You were comfortable. Accessible."

"Accessible? That sounds a little demeaning."

"Just a little? Shit. When that flew out of my mouth, my subconscious was going in for the kill."

He smirked, elbow on the edge of the door, rubbing his thumb on his bottom lip. Had he done that before? At the Palihood house? I didn't remember. He seemed pensive and maybe a little hurt. I felt protective of him, even if I was the one I was protecting him from.

"If it's any comfort, you were the one who hurt me most." I put my hand on his knee. He put his hand over mine and squeezed my fingers together. "After that night, when it was just us, I really started to like you."

"That's no comfort whatsoever."

"Didn't think so."

The rain stopped as if God had flipped a switch. If it were daytime, the sun would have come out.

"I wasn't out to hurt you," he said. "I was out to not get hurt."

"Get off here." I pointed at the exit, holding my next thought until I knew he wasn't going to drift on the slick road. "You know you don't have a case. Your cellist."

"Yeah. I know."

"Make a left here. And you knew I was working in the LA office."

"Read it in the company newsletter. Fine print on the last page. New hires."

"Martin Wright? Does he really think he was ripped off?"

"Every couple of weeks. Especially when he doesn't take his meds."

I closed my eyes and took a deep breath. If I was being honest with myself, I'd known it all along. The case was built out of ice cubes and set on a frying pan. He didn't have to come to Los Angeles for it either. He could have managed the whole thing with faxes. So why? I'd gotten easier to find. There were a few hundred TV channels and libraries had computers now.

Fuck it. He was a goddamn lawyer. He could have found me anytime.

"What do you want?" I asked.

His Adam's apple bobbed down and back up with a deep swallow. He squeezed my fingers again. "Something came across my desk. I don't do international cases, but I was helping an associate, and I saw your name."

"House at the end of the block with the hedge and the gate. Where did you see my name?"

"It wasn't yours. Your family's." He pulled up to the gate and stopped. The gate was closed, and outside his window sat a wet keypad waiting for my code. He put the car in park and shifted to face me. "I didn't think it had anything to do with you. I came to LA to see if you'd thought of me at all. Strat had all the girls. I did all right, but..."

"But? What came across your desk?"

"You were different. Cin—sorry. Margie. I never stopped

134

thinking about you. When I saw your name twice in a month, I had to do something. I should have sent an interoffice or something, but I didn't want to freak you out."

"This has been so much more successful."

"Did you think about me? All that time? The baby—"

"No."

He looked stricken. Or maybe confused. Then he tilted his head a little as if he didn't believe me. Fuck him. But gently and sweetly. Again.

"Between having the baby and crashing into you in the hall, I didn't think about you once."

"Not once?"

"When I read about Strat dying, of course. Sometimes 'Blue Valley' comes on the radio. But otherwise, no. Not really. You haven't even existed to me."

Behind him, a tiny light in the corner of the keypad went from orange to green. The camera was on. There was a disembodied *bleep* a second later.

"Enter my code, or security's going to be out here with an agenda."

He rolled down the window.

"Sorry," I said. "I'm just telling it like it is."

"It's fine." He stuck his hand out the window. If his posture and tone were any indication, it wasn't fine. Not at all. "What's the code?"

"*My* code. We each have our own."

"Okay. What is it?" He looked at me expectantly, fingers poised an inch from the keypad.

I choked back a sob that nearly broke the speed barrier rushing up my throat. "Fifty-one-fifty."

I pressed my lips together to hold it all back and squeezed my eyes shut until little bursts of light exploded in the darkness.

"Just press it," I said, running my words together. "Just do it. I didn't forget you. I thought you didn't want me, and I was okay with that. I just took my lumps, but I think about you every day. Every time there's music anywhere. Jingles in commercials. Muzak in the elevator. You're there, and sometimes you're mocking me and sometimes you're holding me, but you're there. I didn't want you to know that. Ever."

He squeezed my hand, flipped it on his knee, and put our palms together. I didn't open my eyes, just felt him there. Heard the clicks and beeps of the buttons. When I opened my eyes, the windshield was clear, but my vision was fogged.

Drew leaned over and ran his thumb under my eyes. I pushed him away and flipped out his hankie. He smiled. I sniffed as I wiped my face.

"It's okay," he said. "It was a crazy time. We were both kids. And you had a lot on your plate. I should have been there for you."

The gate creaked open. God, the last thing I wanted to deal with was my family.

"I don't know how I feel."

"But you feel something." He rolled up his window.

"Yeah." I sniffed as he pulled forward.

"That was all I wanted to hear. Because I'd hate to think fucking in the front seat of a rental was our last time together."

Drew pulled around the circular drive and planted the Audi close to the front door. The stones were wet and glistening in the front lights. The fountain tinkled, and the spring flowers leaned against the direction of the wind. Cars lined up on each side of the drive, and the valet staff hung out under the eaves.

Harvey, our butler, ran out with a black umbrella and opened my door. "Good evening, Ms. Drazen. I'm afraid they started dinner without you."

"Thanks. It's fine."

"Watch your step."

"It's not raining anymore." I indicated the umbrella.

"There's mist."

I'd grown up with this type of attention and found it was always best to let people do their jobs the best way they knew how.

Drew stood by the trunk of the car, trying to not look off-put by the butler and the huge span of the umbrella. But I knew better. Whenever a regular person saw the Malibu house and the staff, they had to hide their reaction.

I was about to tell Harvey that the fountain sounded louder than usual when Drew looked down. Water was pouring from the trunk.

"Crap," I said, keeping it clean for Harvey. "Aren't these things waterproof?"

Drew didn't know how sensitive the butler was, so he cursed up a storm as he opened the trunk. Three inches of water sat at the bottom, soaking the bottoms of the banker's boxes.

"We'd better bring them in," I said then turned to Harvey. "Can you find us some dry boxes?"

"Indeed."

I took his umbrella, and he dashed inside.

"Well, now your case against Moxie Zee is really dead," I said.

"And to think I was betting my career on this fingerprinting technique."

He picked up a box from the bottom. I held my arms out, and he placed it on them.

"Let's go in the side door. Avoid everyone. This way."

Drew took the second box and closed the trunk. "I was looking forward to meeting your family."

"No, you weren't. Trust me."

I took him to the side of the house, through the five-car garage I rarely saw because we had a valet to move cars around, to the part of the house the eight of us hid out in. The real kitchen. Not the ones the caterers heated up stuff in, the one everyone could see. But the kitchen the cook and his staff used. We curled up in the pantries and cooled off in the walk-in fridge. Sheila had made herself an apprentice and actually learned to cook there.

"Margie!" Orry shouted with a thick French accent, a clump of his grey comb-over flying up as he jogged to me. It looked like a parking barrier going up and down. He'd been our family chef for as long as I could remember.

The kitchen was alive with shouts, flames, *chopchopchop* for the night's dinner.

"Hey." I turned my cheek to him so he could kiss it. "This is Drew. He…" I caught myself. I didn't want to send the staff buzzing. "He works with me."

"Nice to meet you. You're not putting those on my butcher's block."

"I thought your bed would—"

"I'll laugh in advance. You can go in the wine cellar. Shoo. Before Grady forgets the blue in black and blue. *Grady!*" Orry was off, shouting to his grill chef about the temperature of the sea bass. Dad was picky about his blacks and blues.

"You running a restaurant?" Drew asked, juggling the box to keep stuff from falling out the bottom.

"It's Good Friday. Day of fasting and woe followed by gorging on fish. Come on." I jerked my head toward a narrow, half-open door and headed for it. He followed.

The lights were already on, which was good because I didn't have a free hand. We walked carefully down the creaky wood stairs to the cold, dry cellar, into the tasting room. It had only a few racks of seasonal wines that the sommelier decided should be consumed sooner rather than later, clean glasses, a refrigerator for cheese, and a metal table with stools. I put my box on the table, and Drew put his next to mine.

"Feel like a drink?" I said.

"Actually, yes."

I picked up two glasses and a bottle at random while he unloaded a box, laying the masters out in a line. The labels had fallen off.

"Are they ruined?" I asked, popping the cork.

"Yes, but no one cares about Opus 33." He found a file and opened it. Half-wet contracts. Runny-inked documentation. A package of bowstrings. "They must put away anything left in the studio. I had no idea they even cleaned the place. Ever."

He slid the top off the second box. Deep breath. His history was soaked inside.

"Here." I handed him his wine and held mine up for a toast. "To... I don't know what."

"To Stratford Gilliam. May he rest in fucking peace."

We clinked glasses. I looked at him over the rim as I sipped the red nectar. It went right to my head.

Stratford Gilliam.

May he rest in peace.

CHAPTER 28.

1982 – The night of the Quaalude

Six hours before I crawled out from under Indy, I'd been a drug-free virgin. But in the early morning hours after Hawk got kicked out of the house and I fulfilled a fantasy I didn't know I had, I had a sore asshole and a sour feeling in my bones. I'd seen Lynn's grouchy ass after she was luded, and I empathized for the first time.

The Palihood house was dead quiet and lit only by the moon through the windows. I padded to the kitchen naked, bold in my crankiness. I wasn't doing that blue shit again. Feeling scrambled and rancid afterward wasn't worth the happy hornies. I could get horny on my own, thank you. And happy was pure bullshit anyway.

At least that was done. I didn't have a single virgin part of my body anymore.

I filled a glass with water and slogged it. Refilled. Drank. Refilled. Drank more slowly.

The pool lights were on under the perfectly flat bean shape. Maybe a swim would cheer me up. It wasn't until I got to the screen door that I saw the orange pin of a lit cigarette making an arc from Strat's mouth to the side of the couch.

"I hear you, Cin."

"How did you know it wasn't Indy?" I asked from behind the screen.

He arched his back and neck until he could see me. "He walks like a fucking elephant." He lay flat again. "You're naked."

I opened the door. "Yeah. My ass hurts."

"Bad?" He looked over the pool and dragged on his cigarette.

I took his pack off the table. "No. Just irritated." I sat and lit one.

"That can't happen again."

"Did I blow your mind?" I dropped his lighter on the table with a *clickclack*.

"That guy's like my brother. He cares about you. Really cares about you."

He had a towel over his waist, but the rest of him was bare. The musical staffs on his chest rippled. I hadn't tasted them. I hadn't done much of anything but received him. I felt cheated.

"And what about you?" I said.

"He and I have a deal."

"Oh yeah?"

"You're his."

"You flip a coin or something?" I said it without breathing, half joking, half too far on the wrong side of a lude to be anything but negative. I emptied my lungs, letting the nicotine rush make my hands tingle.

"Played a few hands."

"You serious?"

"He pulled a straight."

I leaned back on the couch. "You could have asked me."

He stretched his arm out to the ashtray. The muscles were given definition by the tattoo. What a gorgeous thing he was.

"Nah." He stamped his butt out with a flutter of orange embers. "We didn't want to fight."

"How do you explain your dick in my ass then?"

He shrugged. "One night."

I leaned on the arm of the outdoor couch and stuck my cigarette in my teeth. Fuck them. I wasn't a baseball card to be traded around. "Fuck you guys."

"You did." He got up and stood over me. The towel was gone, and his cock stood straight and hard between us.

"One night," I said. "Did you agree ahead of time?"

"If the situation came up, yeah. That was part of the agreement."

"Fuck you twice." My voice dripped with honey. I hadn't intended it, but the sore feeling in my ass had abated, and the poor judgment of my cunt went live.

We regarded each other, above and below, half-drugged and young, looking for stupid excuses to do stupid things.

"You might get your chance. It's still night."

"For a few hours. Then, yeah, I'm his."

He touched the inside of my knee. No pressure, just a touch. "Open your legs, Cin."

I pulled my knees apart slowly. He kneeled on the couch and spread them, tilting forward to kiss me. He kissed like a man. As if he was marking territory with his tongue. I wrapped my arms around him.

Just once, I told myself. Just the once, I could trade them the way they'd traded me.

I let Strat take me. There was no other way to describe the way he held me down, pushed on my clit until I was close, then slowed down to keep me on the edge, kissing me tenderly right before I came and he exploded inside me.

Only then was I satisfied.

CHAPTER 29.

1994

The wine was going to my head. It seemed as if Drew pulled the Bullets and Blood masters out with special reverence. I'd laid a towel out to soak up the water, and he placed the boxes on them gently.

I was going to have to tell him that the baby that had split us apart might not have been his. We'd been careless with our bodies then.

But when I saw him pull an envelope out of the box and I felt the bond that he'd had with his friend, I felt a real pull to tell him and a stronger pull to just bury it forever. Why bring it up? To what end would I risk hurting him with his friend's betrayal? I didn't fool myself into thinking I meant so much to him that my betrayal was equal to Strat's. The only thing I risked by telling the truth was damaging his memory of his best friend. I didn't want to turn that bond into a lie.

I was a coward. I owed him the truth.

"Drew. Indy... I—"

A young man's voice came from the top of the stairs, yelling in French. Orry shouted back. The door slammed. Feet scuffled along the wood, and a boy barreled into the room, shirt half untucked, ginger hair askew.

"What the—?"

"Jonathan," I said, noticing his frozen, terrified features.

"Margie. When did you get here?"

"This is Drew. He works with me."

They nodded at each other, practically grunting like apes.

145

Little Jon was a man already, too tough for his own good.

"What's wrong?" I said. "You look like you just saw a ghost."

He swallowed. The kids came to the wine cellar when they needed to get away from the bullshit of the huge house. Sometimes to hide. Sometimes to sulk. I knew where to find Fiona during report cards' week, Leanne every twenty-eight days, Carrie whenever Dad was home.

"I'm all right." He started back upstairs.

Drew thumbed through an envelope.

"Wait," I said to Jonathan. "Try this."

I handed him my glass of wine. He was in fifth grade, but he was allowed to sip, and I wasn't ready to let him go back up to whatever was bothering him. He took the glass. Treating him like a grown-up worked, and he seemed calmer when he handed it back.

"It tastes fine," he said.

"Come in the storage room with me for a sec. I want to talk to you. Drew, do you mind?"

"It's fine." He looked up from a wet, runny note for a second and locked eyes on Jonathan.

I thought nothing of it. Not Indy's slack jaw or the way his eyes went a millimeter wider. I just pulled my brother into the inner chamber and sat him on a case of ancient vintage.

"What's wrong?" I whispered.

"Nothing."

"Jon."

"What?"

"Let's be efficient with our time. You're going to tell me. Might as well get it over with."

He pursed his lips, crossed his arms, jutted his jaw. I leaned on a low shelf and waited.

"You can't tell," he said.

"You know I won't."

"You need to really swear."

Jesus. To be in grade school again. To make the big little and the little big. To think you had control when you didn't and adulthood was just childhood layered over with manners and privilege. When lies seemed like easy answers to uncomfortable truths.

"All right," I said. "Let's do this. Let's take a pledge. We hold our hands up and swear anything we say is secret. When we put our hands down, we lock it closed and go back to normal."

He thought about it for a second, then with a short nod he said, "Okay."

"But there's another thing. We cannot lie. Not when the pledge is open."

"Fine."

I held my hand up, and he mirrored me.

"Pledge open," I said. "What happened?"

He took a deep breath and looked at the corner of the room. "Kerry and I were outside when it started raining, and we got stuck in the pool house."

Kerry was the daughter of one of Dad's associates. She was a year older than Jonathan and pretty smart.

"Go on."

"We started doing stuff."

Jesus Christ, use a condom.

He's not ready.

He glanced at me, tearing his attention from the corner for half a second, then planting it back. I didn't answer the glance or egg him on. I knew what was coming, more or less. Mom and Dad weren't very forthcoming about sex with the kids, thinking my early knowledge led to my early downfall.

He spit out the next line. "I think she broke it."

"Broke what?" I knew the answer, but my mouth ran before my brain caught up.

He wouldn't say but pointed at his crotch with both hands.

Do. Not. Laugh. Do. Not. Laugh.

"What makes you think it's broken?"

"She touched it. It got... it got weird then..." He looked at the ceiling.

I had to finish for him. Putting him on the spot wasn't

working. He was in fifth grade, and though he'd started getting big, he was still a child.

"It got hard then felt tickly then white stuff came out?"

His eyes went wide. "Yes."

"It's not broken."

"How do you know?"

"Aren't you and your friends talking about this amongst yourselves? Girls? Sex?"

"I didn't have sex with her!"

I waved it away. "I know. Okay. I'm just going to assure you, it's not broken. You're fine. But tomorrow, let me take you to lunch and I can tell you why. All right?"

He took a deep breath of reprieve. "Yes."

"Until then, keep away from Kerry O'Neill."

"All right."

"Tuck your shirt in."

He did it, jamming the shirttails into his waistband as if Daddy was in the other room. He took a step toward the doorway.

"Jon. Stop."

"What?"

I put my hand up then down. "Close pledge."

"Close pledge."

We went back into the tasting room. Drew leaned on one of the benches, hair flopped over his face like a rock star, shirt dry like a lawyer, with a manila envelope in one hand and a white rectangle in the other. He looked at it then Jonathan.

"What?" I said.

Drew just shook his head as Jonathan bolted up the stairs with barely a wave.

"Strat mailed stuff to Audio City. I don't know why." He put down the manila envelope. Old stamps. Crap handwriting. He laid out the contents. "A note for me, and pictures of when we were kids. He was... he was so hurt. He couldn't show it because you were mine. But..." His voice drifted to silence.

"Drew?"

"When you left, he acted like it was nothing." He pushed

the runny letter toward me.

I couldn't see much but my name, my real one, and phrases... *she was yours but... never wanted this... like a brother to me...*

"I knew about you and Strat. He told me in pledge," Drew said.

"In Nashville."

"Yes, but I—"

"That's why you were such a dick when you got back."

"I regret that."

"I deserved it."

He looked at the picture, shook it, pressed his lips together, and gave it to me as if it was the hardest thing he'd had to do in his life. I took it but kept my eyes on his. I had no idea what he could look so distressed about.

"What is it?" I asked.

"Just tell me what you see."

I looked at the picture.

Two boys about twelve years old, arms over shoulders, a suburban sidewalk stretching behind them. I recognized young Drew McCaffrey by the flop of his hair and the shape of his eyes.

And the other boy? I recognized him. I knew who he was. He was Stratford Gilliam, a kid with only a few more years to live, but that wasn't the kid I recognized. He looked like the three-dimensional kid had been transported from my house onto a two-dimensional surface.

I swallowed. None of this computed.

"It's a coincidence," I whispered.

Not unless Stratford Gilliam fucked your mother.

I couldn't do the math in my head.

Twelve-year-old Strat was a clone of my brother, Jonathan.

No. The other way around. Jonathan looked exactly like Strat.

I looked up from the picture. Drew stood above me, confident and together as if he knew something I didn't.

"Your family name came up in the Dublin office. Your

baby's adoptive family is suing your father for breach of contract."

"I don't understand."

Don't you?

"They never had your real name. I presume it was to protect you. It took that long to find him."

"There would be two babies."

"We checked the public records. Your mother's eighth child was stillborn."

I took a step back, covering my mouth so I wouldn't scream. The calculus suddenly made sense. A sick fucking sense.

"I didn't know what I'd find here," Drew said. "But I didn't think this. I thought it was simpler. Not until I saw—"

I didn't hear anything else. Just my little brother's—

son's

—voice in my head as he spoke French with a perfect ear for tone. As I saw the lines of his body superimposed on Strat's—

his father's

—and the face which was unmistakably from the same gene pool.

I did the math with my senses. Heard the voice and saw the face. Smelled the new baby smell that seemed of my own body and knew, just knew, he was mine.

"I can't." My breathing got choppy. I was shaking.

Drew grabbed my wrists. "Margie."

"I can't tell him."

"You don't—"

"Oh, God."

"*Shh.* It's going to be all right."

He tried to gather me in his arms, but I pushed him away and I ran. I flung myself up the narrow stairs into the chaos of the kitchen. How many people were in the ballroom? Fifty? A hundred?

"Margie?" Orry asked, a piece of raw fish in his thick hands.

Everyone in the kitchen was looking at me, sauté pans frozen mid-agitation, break knives up, colanders dripping starch-thickened water into drains.

I heard Drew clop a couple of elephantine steps up from the cellar.

Cornered.

Your brother is your son.

I didn't even know what I was running from. I was a spider in a tub. I couldn't get up the sides. Couldn't get away, even on eight legs, from the glass bowl coming down.

"Margie?" Drew called.

A second had passed, and in that second, every feeling I was supposed to have in the past few decades dropped on me. I felt my shell break under the pressure as my insides got bigger than my outside, slowly giving way to hairline fractures. I couldn't do this here. I couldn't break with the kitchen staff staring and Drew climbing the stairs.

I ran out of the kitchen, following the map of my childhood.

Through the morning room, the library, the kids' playroom, and the breakfast room to the back deck. I threw myself down the wooden stairs to the beach where I almost collapsed on the cold sand. I got my feet under me and ran toward the wall of sound and water. The horizon. The darkness on the outskirts of the lights of civilization, where the water flattened the land.

I fell with my knees in the water and the rush of the tide in my ears. I stayed there and wept. I wept for what I'd done to sweet Drew. For acting as though Strat had no feelings. For my son who I was never, ever going to hurt by telling. For my misguided parents who had lost a baby and taken mine into their hearts.

The lip of the next wave reached me, soaking my calves and the top of my head. I wasn't mature enough for any of this. No one was. But I didn't cry for myself. I cried for everyone I'd hurt.

The water got louder than I thought possible, blowing at my ears so much that my lungs felt the pain, and the earth went out from under me. I spun in space, clawed the wet sand, tasted rough salt and foam. The sea wrapped around me like a vise, yanking me against it, pulling me to the air, where Drew had me in his arms.

He put me on the sand, and his voice became the sense inside the ocean's chaos. "Margie?"

He was cloudy and grey. My eyes couldn't focus. My chest couldn't hold my lungs, and I coughed. Sucked in a breath. Was I drowning or crying so hard I couldn't breathe?

His hands on my cheeks.

"Talk to me," he said.

"I don't know what to do."

"I know."

"I want to claw my heart out of my chest."

I realized I was gripping the front of my shirt as if I meant to literally claw through skin and bone.

He took my hands, leaning over. "It's all right. Margie. Can you hear me?"

"Yes. I'm sorry. I was young. I put you in a terrible position."

"No. Don't you dare. Don't you ever blame yourself. Ever. I was the one to blame. I should have known better."

"I never admitted I loved you."

"Neither did I."

"I was scared."

"I don't want you to be scared. Not ever again."

I reached for him, and he held me on the beach. I was cold, but I wasn't. I was hurt, but I was healed. I was alone, but no, I wasn't. Not at all. I pressed my face to his neck and let him encircle me so tightly I thought he'd break me.

"I'm so sorry," he said.

I couldn't see his face in the embrace, but mine scrunched with the push of sobs.

"I didn't tell you what I knew the minute I came to LA. I didn't know what I was walking into. I was afraid you'd shut down. I was afraid I'd still have feelings for you. And I do, Margie. I do."

I nodded.

"I know you just got blindsided tonight."

I choked out a laugh. We loosened our hold on each other until we were face to face. I brushed the sand from his cheek.

"Blindsided," I said. "Good word."

"I had no idea. I want you to know. I had pieces but didn't know the puzzle."

I nodded. "No one would believe the truth."

"What should we do?"

I knew he'd asked a broad question. He was talking about us, the world, the firm, my family, our past, our future. But I couldn't think past the tide of feelings. They may have gone back out to sea for the moment, but they'd be back. If I knew anything about emotions (and I didn't know a damn thing but this), they'd be back.

"Let's slip around the side and go to my place," I said.

"You've got a crappy track record of sneaking out of here."

"This time I have you with me."

He smiled and shifted a strand of hair from my face. "You do. You have me."

He kissed me with the passion of a promise. We stood and walked off the beach together.

CHAPTER 30.

1994

Kentucky. More than halfway to New York.

I didn't dig graveyard scenes or talking to guys who weren't really there. I didn't understand putting flowers down for a dead guy who hadn't seemed to like them when he was alive. The young groupie hated downer shit, and the jaded law clerk—no, lawyer—didn't have the time.

And there was still the whole issue of feelings.

I told Drew when he opened the car door for me, "Doing something for the express purpose of making yourself feel sad is fake. The thing is fake, and the feeling is fake."

"The lawyer doth protest too much."

He held his hand out for me, and I took it, letting him pull me out of the car. I didn't need help, but he liked helping. Didn't take me long to figure that out, and who was I to refuse him his pleasure?

He'd given me too much in the past six months. He'd stood by my decision to let Jonathan stay my brother, to let my parents think I knew nothing about their loss. Though my father had masterminded the entire fairytale, his scheme to keep his grandson in the family was meant to protect my mother.

I couldn't refuse my father that, but mostly, I remained silent to protect my son, Jonathan. I'd die with that secret. I'd sew my own mouth shut before letting it pass my lips.

The only other person who knew was the man holding the flowers in the parking lot of a Kentucky cemetery.

The little notes all over my house were long gone.

"I'll end you," I whispered to Drew one night, wrapped in sheets and darkness, my voice shredded from crying his name too many times.

He kissed me. I could taste my pussy on his face.

"You always threaten me before you fall asleep."

That was when the worry swept in. The worry that my family would be upended. That my brother would lose his mind. That my mother would go off the deep end. And my father, ever unpredictable, would hurt the messenger if the messenger wasn't me.

"You're the only one who knows." I touched his face in the dark. "I trust you. But I will end you."

He pinned my hands over my head. "I'll end you too."

We'd had this discussion a hundred times. In bed, over dinner, in earnestness and in jest. "I'll end you" wasn't a threat. Not really. It was a way of telling him how deeply I trusted him.

"Not if I end you first," I said, pushing my hips against him.

"How are you going to do that, Cinny-sin-sin?"

"Test me."

He let my hands go and wrapped himself around me. "Never."

"Smart guy."

He didn't move and barely paused. "Come back to New York with me. I can't live without you. The city feels like a tomb."

I sighed. We'd been long distance for too many months. "Speaking of testing… I'm sitting for the bar in August."

He got up on his elbows, eyes wide and blue, shocked and delighted. I'd waited to tell him so I could drink in that expression.

"The New York State Bar?" he asked.

"No, asshole, the old man's bar on Seventh and B. Of course the New York State Bar."

He was off me like a shot, sitting straight, suddenly awake. "You have to study. Have you been studying? We have to get on it."

"Relax. It's easy."

He scooped up my entire body and covered it in happy kisses.

I hadn't forgotten what had brought us together, but it was all drowned out by a feeling of safety and joy. I had to admit, as feelings went, those were pretty good.

The parking lot of the Kentucky cemetery was empty but for a few beat-up trucks. Our shiny black Audi was the brightest object for miles. Drew had parked it in the middle of the lot, away from the wooden poles poking out from the earth at odd angles. The rusted chains between them were shaped like kudzu-wrapped smiles, one after the other on the edge of the rectangle—smile, smile, smile. The sky was the color of the asphalt, and the freight train clacking at the river's edge lumbered slowly, as if showing off its eternal length like a peacock showing off his blues.

I'd passed the New York bar six months after passing the California bar. I threatened to rack up forty-eight more states for fun, and Drew threatened to tie me to the bed.

That had worked out well.

Everything had worked out well. I was leaving. Maybe for a few years, maybe for good, but I was going. I never imagined I'd leave Los Angeles, but the thought of such freedom made me feel silly and lighthearted.

Me. Margaret Drazen.

I got goofy in the weeks before we finally left. Daddy hadn't been happy when we told him, and he eyed Drew as if maybe he remembered him from twelve years before, when a young man had shown up at the door asking for his oldest daughter.

But, you know, tough shit.

When Drew insisted we take 70 (apparently, I wasn't supposed to say *the* 70. Just 70 without the article), I didn't think anything of it. But he swung off the interstate and went south into Kentucky.

"Six-oh-six E-Y-E-B-R-O-W," I said from the passenger seat.

He glanced over. "I need to."

"I know."

We stopped at a light and he put his hand over mine. "I went to the funeral, but I didn't visit the... you know. The thing." He looked away.

"There's a florist up ahead. You don't want to show up empty-handed."

He'd bought a bunch of yellow flowers because they looked fresher than any of the others. Stillness shrouded us on the way to the cemetery. I pressed my hand on his, rubbing the rough patch on his fingertip where guitar strings had calloused the skin.

I took his hand again in the parking lot, and we walked down the gravel path, counting lanes and ways against our printed map.

We found the grave exactly where it was supposed to be. Just another stitch in the houndstooth pattern of grey stones on the grassy hill. It said what it was supposed to say. His name. The relevant dates. Where the others had their defining roles—Father, Wife, Mother, Son, Baby—Stratford Gilliam had a clef like the one on his neck, short five-line staff and a quarter note tucked between the two lowest lines.

"I feel stupid," he said. "It's just a rock and dirt."

"Yeah. It's stupid."

That was why we were together. We shared a cold,

calculating cynicism. We were immune to sentiment.

"I like the musical note," I said. "It's cute."

"I picked it. I drew it for his dad and faxed it over."

"Really?"

"Yeah. It's…" He swallowed hard. "It's F. The note." He blinked. Smiled with his lips tight in a thin line. "It's so dumb." His voice cracked.

"I bet."

He looked away from the grave and shut his eyes. "I picked F for…" He shook his head, shot a little laugh that was sticky with sadness. "Friend. I needed it to be F for friend. Like I was in kindergarten."

I put my hand on his cheek, thumb under his eye, ready to catch the tears that I knew were coming. "I'm embarrassed for you."

He opened his eyes. So blue. Bluer than the cloud-masked sky that day. He wasn't the man I'd met so long ago. The musician on the edge of fame. So close to the dream. So close he could save the world with it.

But he was. That man was still in him. Sometimes I forgot about that twenty-year-old with the potential he had a lifetime to fulfill.

He laid the flowers down. I rubbed his guitar callouses as we walked back to the car.

"You should play music again," I said.

"No."

"You're not doing him any favors."

"It's not about Strat."

That was a lie, but I couldn't prove it.

"You're right. The world is better off without you making music."

He laughed a little and wrapped his arm around my neck, pulling me close and kissing the top of my head.

"I mean it," I said. "You're sexy with a guitar. Chicks dig it."

"You sure you could stand the competition?"

"Have you met me? I don't have competition." I walked

backward in front of him, each of my hands in his. "You don't have to be a rock star. Just write some songs. See how it sounds. You might like it." I bit my lower lip. "I might like it. I could be your groupie all over again. I'll let you fuck me if you play."

He pulled me to him. "You're going to let me fuck you whether I play or not."

"I hear South Dakota has the easiest bar exam in the country."

"I'm not moving to South Dakota."

"Then you better get that guitar out, Indiana McCaffrey."

"You're threatening me," he growled with a smile. "You know what that does to me."

"What?" I reached between his legs, and we laughed.

I ran back to the car, and he chased me, pinning me to the driver's side door with his kiss. I pushed my fingers through his hair, pulling him closer. I wanted to crawl inside him and live there forever.

He ripped his face away from mine long enough to speak. "I love you, Cinnamon. You're too precocious. Too smart. Too much of a pain in the ass, and I love you."

"Even in South Dakota?"

"I'll play again!" He laughed. "I'll play if you love me."

"You bet your ass I love you."

"Case closed." He kissed me again, pushing me hard against the car with the force of his erection pressed against me.

I groaned into his mouth.

"There was a hotel behind that florist." He spoke in gasps. "Wanna go make the bed squeak?"

"Yes."

We kissed again with an urgency that defied logic, as it should.

The freight train finally lumbered away, the bell on the last car dinging in victory. On the other side of the tracks, the rolling hills dissolved into infinity, and we drove right into it.

The End

Read the story of Jonathan that starts in BEG,
Episode one of the Submission Series.

Thank you for reading.

If you have any questions or concerns, please contact cdreiss.writer@gmail.com

You can join my fan groups:
Goodreads: bit.ly/1klDF9g
Faceboob: www.facebook.com/groups/songsofsubmission/

Or get on the mailing list!